"BARTON!"

On the screen was what Barton had come to think of as the twitchy lobster, the one that didn't look quite like the rest.

"Barton," it said. "This is Shiewen. You musht lishen to me!"

"Doktor Siewen? I don't believe it. Throw that damn hood back and let me see you."

As the hands came up and the hood went back, Barton heard a ghost voice: Doktor Siewen's. *"They catch people and turn them into Demu."*

Other SIGNET Science Fiction You'll Want to Read

Cage a Man

by
F. M. BUSBY

A SIGNET BOOK
NEW AMERICAN LIBRARY
TIMES MIRROR

To Elinor

SIGNET, SIGNET CLASSICS, SIGNETTE, MENTOR AND PLUME BOOKS
are published by The New American Library, Inc.,
1301 Avenue of the Americas, New York, New York 10019

FIRST PRINTING, MAY, 1974

1 2 3 4 5 6 7 8 9

PRINTED IN THE UNITED STATES OF AMERICA

PART I:

A Cage There Was

The ceiling above him was low and gray; Barton's first thought was, What am I doing in the drunk tank? On second thought it didn't stink like a drunk tank, and Barton was far enough awake to know that he was not hung over. So he sat up and looked around. The first thing he noticed was that he was naked, along with everybody else. If this were a drunk tank, it had to be the first coeducational nude drunk tank in his limited experience.

He could make no guess as to where he was, or why. Presumably there was some other place he'd rather be, somewhere he belonged—but when he tried to think of one he drew a blank. Briefly, he wondered why the lack didn't bother him.

He seemed to be the only person awake; at least no one else was sitting up. Looking, Barton estimated about fifty persons sprawled in the room, neither crowded nor widely separated in a space about twenty-five feet square. He stood, and found the ceiling claustrophobically low: not much over six feet, clearing his head by a few inches but heavy-heavy-hanging over it. He didn't like that.

Floor and walls were gray, as well as the ceiling. Solidly. There were no openings that he could see, anywhere. There was light, a little yellowish, but no visible sources; the light was simply there. The gray surfaces were not luminous and the air did not glow. Barton skipped that; it wasn't important. What was important was that he had to take a leak.

No place. He stepped gingerly over and around the sleeping bodies, noting little about them except that they breathed. When he accidentally touched one, it was warm. The floor was at body temperature also, with a slight degree of "give." After exploring the room thoroughly, Barton was faced with the fact that it was not only solid but seamless. Yet the air (warm, like the floor) was fresh and clean. It seemed to move against him gently from all directions, though he could detect no gross air currents.

He still had to pee. Going to one corner of the room, he considerately rolled the nearest occupant out of splashing range and faced the corner. At first he couldn't do it; all the times he'd stood in line (at theaters during intermission, at overcrowded facilities in tourist haunts), with impatient others waiting behind him, came up to clamp the sphincter tight. Waiting, he finally relaxed and the flow came. The interesting thing was that at the floor it simply disappeared: no splash or gurgle. The floor might as well not have been there. It looked dry, felt dry (Barton felt it) and had no telltale smell at all (Barton smelled it).

He had a sudden wild thought that perhaps the whole room was an illusion, and gathered a few bruises trying to launch himself through the floor, a wall, and even the ceiling, before he decided that in this case liquids had certain advantages over solids. His guess might be wrong, he knew, but that didn't mean it was stupid.

Other people were beginning to wake, sit up and even move around. Barton realized that he hadn't paid enough attention to the resident population, of which he was perhaps 2 percent. So he stood quietly in his corner and looked.

The people ranged from ordinary to exotic, in Barton's view. Some were as usual as anyone can be among some fifty naked persons in a sealed room. Others were notable for such things as highly stylized patterns of tattooing, possible cosmetic surgery, and selective depilation. Still others, Barton thought, must have come out of a freak show. Some of them he found hard to believe, but there they were. The frightening thing, though, was that these people were beginning to speak among themselves, and while Barton spoke French and a little German, and could recognize several other languages, he heard not one familiar word from anyone near him. Well, yes—there was one over there!

"Anybody here speak ENGLISH?" he bawled out suddenly. From the far side of the room came a "YES." Accented, but unmistakable. Barton began shouldering his way toward the sound, shouting "ENGLISH" now and then as a navigational aid.

"English" turned out to be a Doktor Siewen, a tall wiry man with a great bushy shock of white hair, and some alarming ideas. He and Barton traded names and shook hands, the ritual prelude to any constructive activity between strangers.

"I know considerable languages, Barton," said Siewen, "and some of them I hear in this place, but not many. Also I hear people talking in languages I didn't think exist."

"I thought I knew a lot of ethnic types, myself, but some of these people don't look like anything I've ever seen, even in pictures."

"There is also that," Doktor Siewen began, but just then he and Barton were knocked apart. A woman pushed between them; two men were chasing her. There were strangenesses about all three. One man caught her; the two sank to the floor together in tight embrace. But the second man came upon them, kicking and clawing; soon all three were battling viciously. Barton wasn't sure whose side the woman was on.

He started to say something to Siewen, but a great feeling of heaviness came over him. His legs collapsed; the impact half-stunned him. He rolled over painfully, and was able to see that nearly everyone else was on the floor also. The heaviness increased.

"This tells us where we are, Barton," Doktor Siewen said, in great strain. "Or where we are not. You know what is this? Artificial gravity, it has to be."

Barton tried to shake the moths out of his brain. "How about just straight acceleration? I mean, on a spaceship thing you could get that, couldn't you?"

"On a spaceship with a room this big," said Siewen, "who could bother to disturb the navigation, only to stop a little squabble in the zoo?" The heaviness increased into blackout . . .

Barton ached all over; someone was shaking him by the

shoulder. "Wake up, Barton; wake up." It had to be Doktor Siewen, unless the whole thing had been a bad dream, so Barton opened his eyes. It hadn't been a dream, or else it still was. Standing beside Siewen was a woman, not like any Barton had ever seen. Barton stood up; she was taller than he and very slim.

"Barton, this is Limila," Siewen said. "You can see, she is not the type human we grow on our world." Limila smiled; her teeth were small, and by Barton's standards, too many. She held out a hand for him to shake; it had an extra finger. A glance downward showed a pair of six-toed feet. The nails of both toes and fingers were thick and pointed, clawlike.

"Hello, Barton. Yes?" she said.

"Hello, Limila. Yes." Her hair was odd. It was perfectly good shiny black hair, twisted up into a knot at the crown of her head, but forward of her ears it did not grow. The front hairline began above one ear and went straight up and over to the other; Barton recalled an old movie of Bette Davis playing Queen Elizabeth I. In compensation, at the back it grew solidly down to the base of the neck. Like she's slipped her wig, Barton thought before he got his thoughts back on track. "Where's she from, Doc?"

"We can't yet talk such technical data," Siewen said. "But Limila has been captured a longer time, was in another group with English-speakers, has fantastic talent of linguistics to learn as far as she has."

"Does she—" He turned to Limila. "Do you know what any of this is all about?" Her breasts were wrong. Not in shape, but set very low and wide on the ribcage.

"We are have by the Demu, I think," she said. "No one know what happen then. No one came back." She looked away, her eyes half-closed, apparently losing interest in the discussion.

"What's a Demu?" Barton asked. She didn't answer, and in a moment walked away.

"Now what's wrong with *her?*"

"We were talking before," Siewen said. "You were not awake for a long time, Barton; finally I worried you were not all right. But Limila told me of the Demu. Likely she did not feel to repeat herself.

"The Tilari, Limila's people, have star travel," he continued. "They are not what you call easy to the mark. They trade with other races and have respect from all. But the Demu raid the Tilari or anyone else; they take people and there is the end of it. They come from nowhere and go back the same way."

"Hell, somebody must know something about them," Barton growled. He was getting a little tired of being told how invincible the Demu were, because he didn't want to have to believe it.

"They are seldom seen. They have unconsciousness devices, which also derange memory function for a time, and other ways not to be noticed. They could have slept everyone here without the gravity if wanting to; that likely was for threat, to make us to behave better."

"Or maybe just plain sadism," Barton said. "I think I'd like to meet one of them sometime without his magic gadget. Anybody know what they look like?"

"A small ship of them, raiding scout perhaps, crashed on Tilara very long time ago. All were killed. The Tilari just began to study the wreck and the dead ones; then must have come another ship. The wreck and dead ones gone, also all but two Tilari in the study group. The two had gone for food supplies and needed instruments."

"At least somebody lucked out," Barton said. "So what's *their* report?"

"I said, a long time ago, Barton. It is all vague, very vague by now; Limila has only read it in her schooling as a child.

"She says they were roughly human shape and size. Hard like stone to the touch. She thinks they have not the features of face and other things real people have. But the Demu think *they* are the only real people."

"How can anybody know that?"

"Demu picture record, seen by the two Tilari not taken," said Siewen. "With sound-capsules, from which their name Demu is learned. By reports, showed unmistakably Demu in relation to other races as people to animals."

Barton didn't answer; the concept angered him. The phrase "hard like stone" stuck in his mind; he had the impression he'd cracked open quite a few rocks in his time, for one reason or another. His memory was vague but the picture of a fossil fern came to him, and the smell of a campfire. A field trip?

"Anything else Limila knows about them?"

"Legend, folklore, from other peoples made victims. They take you, they use you as domestic animal; maybe eat you."

"Seems like a long haul to the meat market," Barton said. "Wouldn't it be easier to breed their own stock from what they get on the first raid?"

"As I say, Barton: folklore. But the great fear is not of being killed or even eaten. There is a story so old, the race that first told it is extinct. By supernova, long past. This is, the goal of the Demu is to make animals into people."

"I don't get you."

"If I have it, they catch people to try to turn them into Demu."

"Oh, come off it, Doc! How could that be?"

"I don't know; Limila doesn't know. But it is said on many worlds."

"So's a lot of other horse-puckie, I imagine." The subject had no handle he could grasp. He began stretching and bending, working the aches out of his muscles. Doktor Siewen shrugged and said nothing more.

Limila was back. She started to say something, but an excited babble broke out across the room and cut her off in midsentence. Barton wheeled to see what was going on.

The walls were leaking. At intervals, small jets of liquid spurted at a height of about five feet. Barton realized he was deadly thirsty. He wasn't alone; there was a rush. Barton held back for a moment but decided that if the Demu wanted to poison them, the air supply would be simpler.

The water was cool with a slight mineral taste, not unpleasant. Then it changed; the liquid became thicker and milk-colored. Just like Instant Breakfast, Barton thought, except not sweetened. He found he was hungry, too.

The stuff stopped coming before he'd had enough of it, but he could feel relief from the low blood-sugar condition he hadn't consciously noticed. Barton felt a little more as if he might have some sort of chance in this game after all. He realized it was silly to feel that way from a mere shot of nutriment at the whim of his unseen captors. But what the hell . . .

He turned from the wall, looking for Siewen or Limila. The other people of non-Earth origin began to register with him. They hadn't necessarily had surgery or depilation or tattooing, he saw now; they were simply different by nature. Some weren't all that different; some were hard to accept. He decided to work his attitudes out later when he had the time for it. When things weren't so crowded, if ever. What he really wanted to do was sit down with his back to a corner and feel less vulnerable, but his fellow captives shared his preference for using the corners of the room as urinals; they were all in use.

He noticed a discrepancy, and the vagrant thought crossed his mind: That's funny; I don't *feel* constipated. Then he saw Siewen and moved across the room to join him.

Their discussion brought no new information or ideas. Barton got tired of standing or sitting; he lay down and dozed off. Having his back against the wall was better than no shelter at all.

Barton was having a good dream; it got better when he woke up. Limila was all over him. What she had in mind was obvious, and Barton found that he had no objections. But first he pulled them both up sitting, looking at each other; he wanted to see her fully as a person.

Her hair was down and loose; there was a lot more of it than he would have expected. Her features were so lean and delicate as to be almost harsh, but her face had beauty to him, once he was used to its not stopping at the forehead. Her eyes were the color of liquid mercury, with more iris and less white than seemed reasonable. And her lips curved sweetly as she smiled.

He must have looked for longer than he knew, because she said, "Will we now?" Barton didn't answer in words. He found some differences in the way things were angled and the way some muscles worked, but he had no complaints.

Not much later he was startled to find that Limila was on the same friendly terms with Doktor Siewen, but Bar-

ton was realist enough not to try to impose his own
ideas on a lady he didn't understand more than about 5
percent, if that. In the way he had now, he put everything
out of his mind but the moment. In fact, some hours later,
he and Limila were exchanging pleasured smiles when he
felt the blackness of approaching unconsciousness. There
wasn't even time to kiss.

The next time Barton woke, he was alone. The quali-
ties of the room were the same but this one was smaller,
about ten feet square. Not exactly ten feet, not exactly
three meters, not exactly any measurement Barton was
familiar with—and Barton knew he was capable of estimat-
ing dimensions quite closely. The gray surfaces, the low
ceiling, the temperature, the light with no sources or shadows, the floor and walls you could piss through but not
escape through—these were all the same. But the feel of
the place was that of a solid planet, not a spaceship.
There was nothing more, just Barton, alone in his room.
This, he realized, is how to go crazy.

Barton was of no mind to go crazy. He felt he might
be a little bit crazy already, but he didn't intend to let
it go any further than he could help. He still knew only
a little of what he was up against; as a matter of sur-
vival he set out to learn more. The effort kept his mind
occupied, and he figured that was all to the good.

Over an unmeasured period of time he discovered
several things. His solid wastes, infrequent on his present
diet, also went through the floor without trace, but not
instantaneously; they sank gradually, leaving no residue.
The room reserved one corner of itself for these functions; it told Barton so with electrical shocks.

His food and water, neither separate nor appetizing,
rose through another area of the floor in the same way,
the floor forming itself into a sort of cup or bowl to hold
the liquid mush. The intervals between meals were irregular and unpredictable. When Barton got angry at an
especially long delay and pissed in the bowl when it appeared, the room left the mess with him for several
hours before removing it and providing his next feeding.
He didn't foul his food again. Frustrated out of his

mind, Barton was, but not of a mood to let himself be stupid.

There wasn't much that he could learn from his limited environment, but he tried. With the constant illumination and irregular feeding schedule, there was no way to tell time. Barton first tried a makeshift count of his own pulse, but aside from the variation with his emotions, he invariably lost track of the thousands. He tried to keep a record of his own waking periods, and had no better luck. The walls and floors would not retain marks. When he tried to lay out hairs or nail bitings on the floor or glue them to the walls with spittle, they simply vanished, usually while he was asleep, though once he saw an attempted marker absorbed into a wall. He shouted and struck at it at the last, which did no good either.

Barton knew he was a little off his head when he began trying to make permanent marks on his own body to keep the one count that meant anything to him: the number of his waking periods. He tried gouging his skin with his fingernails but found his healing rate was accelerated; he could not produce scars. He tried biting himself and was dissuaded by a series of shocks from the floor. The room allowed him to pluck marker stripes through his body hair, but the process was tedious and the result impermanent. He abandoned the effort and gave himself up to the sulks.

Once in a blank reverie he found himself pulling at his whiskers, and suddenly realized he had had a rough time measurement at hand all along. He pulled one hair from his sprouting beard; the length of it told him he had been caged for about four months, give or take a couple of weeks. His next period of sleep was more relaxed than any since this whole thing had started. Since Before.

Before! Barton hadn't thought of Before, more than fleetingly, since he had wondered what he was doing in the drunk tank. How could he? There was nothing but Here, and Here was so terrible and so frustrating that he couldn't put his attention fully on anything else. And for a time, he hadn't been able to remember very much, anyway.

He woke thinking of Before, though, and wondering about it. His emerging memories were still incomplete. The condition didn't bother him because he didn't recall any better one, except vaguely.

He knew that he had been born in 1945 and was pretty sure he'd been thirty-two at his last birthday. He was an only child, perhaps a little too smart for his own good in the childhood jungle of school, he recalled. Stubborn, somewhat of a loner in his teens. But not much of a rebel at home, or in two years of liberal-arts studies at the local university.

Then the war in Vietnam. He'd panicked and shot a scrawny kid who didn't have a grenade after all, just a small clay jar of oil. Later he'd shot one of his own squadmates who had begun to spray a village with submachine fire; no one could prove it on him for sure, so he didn't get court-martialed. Barton had never told anyone about these things; he'd just lived with them.

He hadn't tried hard drugs, just dew and hash sometimes, so when his hitch was finished he had no trouble getting home and out of the service. But he couldn't get along with his parents anymore. They kept trying to put him back in the little-boy bag and it didn't fit. He knew they loved him but he couldn't take the way they showed it.

Barton went back to college on the G.I. Bill. He wasn't doing well with people, he felt, so he undertook the study of things; he became a physics major. He would have preferred paleontology—he enjoyed fossil-hunting—but there wasn't any money in it and he'd been broke long enough. He was good enough at his studies to graduate with honors. He had about eight to ten dates per school year but got laid once a month by a friendly-mannered professional. As a matter of fact he liked the part-time whore, personally, better than he liked the coeds he dated. Barton felt that he knew honesty when he met it. On the dating scene he hadn't found enough to notice.

After graduation, Barton took a Master's degree and then a job with a company that gave him time to work on his Ph.D. on the side. It seemed to be a good deal, and for the most part, it was. Except for the red tape, which started strong and kept growing.

Just before leaving school, Barton had met a girl who frankly admitted she liked getting laid, and proved it.

Her name was Ada Rongen; she was nearly Barton's height, and slim. She had green eyes, long red hair and a crooked nose from having played shinny at the age of ten. Barton proposed on their third date; they were married in time to avoid a fourth one.

For the most part, over the next few years Barton liked his job and his studies and his marriage. He enjoyed his hobby, oil painting. When the package came apart on him, it did so all at once.

The red tape on Barton's job had piled up until it took nearly half of what should have been productive time. He got clobbered in his Ph.D. Orals by a professor whose main gripe seemed to be that Barton had never taken the prof's own pet course. And he found that Ada's liking for getting laid was not exclusively in his favor.

The day he came home from the Orals fiasco she told him she was pregnant. Then she said, "I think you should know; the child is probably not yours."

Barton didn't ask who, how or why. He moved out. From the job, from the school and from Ada. First he told her to go ahead with a divorce; he'd give her any grounds she needed. " . . . and don't say anything. I've never hit a woman in my life and I don't want to spoil my record." She nodded, silenced by the look of the man who had always been gentle to her.

He moved into a walk-up room and concentrated on his painting. A little of his work began to sell, but mostly he lived on the refund from the company's retirement plan. He picked up, on a part-time basis, with the young sales-girl at the gallery that handled his paintings. And once divorced, he found that without bitterness he could share Ada's eclectic enjoyment of casual sex. They became fairly good friends, in bed and out.

A year or two had gone by like this, a comfortable vegetative time. Painting, drinking with Ada and turning on with Leonie the salesgirl, being lover to each of them in a friendly noncompetitive way. By the time his retire-ment money ran out he could almost but not quite make a living from the painting. He made up the difference with a part-time scut job at the gallery; Barton's tastes, when he so chose, could be relatively inexpensive. He was drifting and he knew it; what better way to spend the dregs of his youth?

And then somehow, at no specific point he could recall, Barton had been torn away from that placid half-remembered existence. To wake up in a gray, seamless cage.

Thinking back, then, Barton lay supine on the gray floor and for the first time in his new existence masturbated slowly and luxuriously, building his urge almost to the deathwish-point of convulsions before he gave himself release. Then, relaxed, he wondered why in hell he had taken so long to think of such an obvious answer to his tensions. The relaxation carried through all that waking period and into sleep.

For the first time Here, Barton woke almost happy, smiling in reminiscence and anticipation. He ate in no great hurry, voided, thought vaguely and with only faint regret on what he could remember of Before. Then he lay down, arranged himself comfortably and thought of pleasure.

Nothing worked. No thoughts, no touch produced the slightest response. There was no doubt in Barton's mind what had happened. The room had noticed that he had discovered a source of pleasure, and turned it off.

That was the first time Barton tried to find a way to kill himself.

He couldn't; the room wouldn't let him. When he tried to do any real damage such as biting at an artery, the room jarred him out of it with electrical shock or radical variations of the gravity, temperature or air pressure, until he gave up and lay cursing, or sometimes crying.

The room had taken a long time to notice that Barton needed a bath or its equivalent. He was getting pretty stinking; his skin was spotted with inflamed areas and mild infections. Then suddenly he began to receive treatments he really didn't appreciate too much. Barton decided the method was probably ultrasonics.

At any rate, the outer layer of his skin flaked off in patches, and so did much of his hair, quite roughly and unevenly. He didn't have a mirror, but by the feel of himself he knew he looked like bloody hell. Furthermore, his beard "calendar" was shot down.

So when Barton one "morning" woke to find one wall no longer gray but looking like a window, with people or something else looking in at him, he was more angry than curious. At first he paid little attention to the appearance of those outside, although they certainly didn't look especially human. But at that point he didn't give a damn whether school kept or not; he was more concerned with what these beings had done to his own looks and functions than with what *they* might happen to look like. What he wanted was a little action.

He did all the standard things: he shouted, made faces, waved his arms and beat on the window. The people (or something) showed no reaction, except now and then to turn to one another and exchange comments. Or apparently so: he couldn't be sure; there was no sound.

When his mainspring ran down, Barton realized that he had better pay attention. Here was a chance for knowledge; it might not last.

What he saw was a group of robed cowled figures, vaguely human-shaped and apparently human-sized. Of course, he thought, this could be closed-circuit TV and not a window at all; in that case the apparent size wouldn't mean much. But Limila had said the Demu were about the size of humans.

Besides gray robes and hoods, he saw shadowed faces and occasional glimpses of hands that didn't have enough fingers. The faces didn't show him a lot. Heavy hairless brow-ridges hid the sunken eyes. There was no nasal ridge, only close-set nostril-holes a little below the eyes. The lips were deeply serrated—like a zipper without the handle, he thought wryly. The whole effect was rather chitinous, like the body shell of a boiled crab and with the same ivory-tinged-with-red color. If there were ears, the hoods covered them. There was no sign of hair, fur or feathers. Hell, not even scales; he wondered if a snake would seem more alien to him, or less, than these creatures. "Demu?" he thought. "They look like a bunch of overgrown lobsters to me!"

One of them stepped forward and gestured to him. Yes, the hand had only three fingers, plus an oversized thumb

set at an odd angle. No fingernails. The gestures carried
no meaning to Barton; in return he thumbed his nose at
the alien, who conferred with the two others before turning again to repeat the movements.

Barton knew what he wanted, now. He paid no heed to
what the other did, but repeated over and over a simple
gesture of throwing back a hood and dropping a robe,
followed by throwing his arms wide in exhibition. The result was another conference among part of his viewing
public. Eventually one of the lobsters stepped close to the
window or screen and pushed the hood back, exposing its
head.

It was about what Barton had expected. The head and
neck looked crustacean; he was sure he was viewing an
exoskeletal being. There were no external ears, but
slightly flanged earholes not much displaced from the human position. The mouth, when open briefly, showed no
teeth and a short stumpy tongue. The skull was slightly
broader than deep, Barton thought, but couldn't be sure
since the creature did not turn to full profile. The neck
was thick and continued the chitinous look. Barton couldn't
tell about the hands, when they reached up to replace
the hood; perhaps the chitin was more flexible there.

Barton kept making doff-the-robe gestures but the up-
front lobster ignored his movements and repeated a gesture
of its own, with one hand in front of the middle of its
robe. Suddenly Barton realized that the creature was pan-
tomiming masturbation. He spat on the window, went to
the far side of the room and curled up facing the wall.
But as he did so, he felt unmistakable signs that his sexu-
ality was working. Then, abruptly, it turned off again. He
couldn't imagine how the lobsters could control him in
that aspect. Some sort of subsonics? Induced brain waves?
Hell, *he* didn't know. He tried to think in terms of
physics, but the concepts seemed dim and jumbled in his
mind. However, he did give some thought to the proper-
ties of the exoskeleton in combat.

For one thing, assuming the creatures were approximately his own size and operating in the same gravity
field, the outer shell had to be light in weight. It would
have great tensile strength and good resistance to com-
pressive loads along a limb segment. But given a little

leverage, Barton thought, it should bend and crumple
like so much macaroni. He hoped with considerable gusto
for a future chance to check his hypothesis; he was still
thinking about it when he went to sleep.

Barton was next awakened by a metallic jangling sound,
like a gong made of chain mail. The wall was a window
again (or TV screen, he reminded himself), with one
robed lobster facing him and gesturing. It might have
been the same one or it might not; Barton couldn't tell
for sure. But from the one-handed gestures and a stirring
in Barton's groin, the creature obviously wanted Barton to
demonstrate autoeroticism.

Well, the hell with that. He'd done it once and they'd
turned him off for it. In return, Barton made throw-off-
that-robe motions. If I have to be a solo whore, he
thought, I'll get paid for it. In knowing a little more what
it's all about. The session ended with no sale when the
window turned back into a gray wall. This time they left
him turned on, but feeling stubborn, he ignored the
possibilities.

The dickering was repeated each waking period. Sometimes there would be only one robed chitinous alien,
sometimes several. Occasionally there was one in the back-
ground that unlike the rest seemed nervous and twitchy,
moving back and forth. Although he couldn't get a good
look, it seemed to Barton that the twitchy one didn't
have quite the same chitinous sheen as the others, though
the features (or lack thereof) were much the same.

Throughout this period of silent bargaining sessions,
Barton took a perverse pleasure in refusing himself any
sexual release except for the involuntary nocturnal type
that occasionally caught up with him. He had thought to
huddle up facing away from the window and do it himself,
but suddenly realized that all four walls and maybe the
floor and ceiling could be one-way windows. Certainly
the lobsters had turned him off before he'd seen any wall
as other than gray and opaque. The hell with them, Barton
felt. At this point, he realized, he might cheerfully have
cut off his nose to spite his face, given the proper tools
for the job. He almost had to laugh.

And yet Barton felt aggrieved when the silent arguments ended, when the walls stayed gray and no robed

lobsters tried to gesture him into doing anything. During his first waking period without such an interview he was subjected to an ultrasonic "bath" of such vigor as to shake nearly every dead cell off him, leaving him not only stone-bald but also tenderly shallow of skin and with thin nails on toes and fingers, not to mention a filling or two that resonated painfully. Barton took this as a display of temper on the part of his personal number-one lobster and set in his mind the goal of someday repaying that entity in kind as best he might. Thereafter the ultrasonics were mild, shaking loose only extraneous matter. Barton theorized that a different lobster had taken charge of his cage.

Going by the length of his regrowing beard, Barton figured it to be nearly a year before he had any further interaction with the outside of the room, other than exchanging food for wastes and an occasional light ultrasonic "bath." Then one "day" he was sitting in a corner staring at the intersection of two walls and the floor, hallucinating. He was hallucinating a great deal at that time; he had found the practice a considerable help to personal peace of mind.

At the moment he was sitting on soft grass at the top of a rounded hill under warm sunlight, facing a slim girl with long red hair. Between them was a cloth laden with a picnic lunch. The girl's nose began to develop a crooked outline; absent-mindedly he thought it straight. They sipped from cold moisture-beaded cans of beer and toasted each other, smiling. A light breeze brought the scent of flowers. He had to straighten her nose again; it wouldn't stay put. He noticed movement far down the hill at the edge of a swamp. Insects, huge yellow-jacketed wasps, were buzzing around a cage. In the cage was a robed hooded lobster that flailed its arms at the wasps. He smiled and watched low-lying smog drift in across the swamp. Then—

He felt a slight "pop" in his ears, as in change of altitude. At first he thought it was part of his hallucination, but on second thought it didn't fit, so gradually he took his attention from inside himself and put it outside, slowly rising and turning from the corner to look at the room overall.

A sort of dome had appeared in the middle of the floor. Yeh; air displacement popped my ears, he thought, and wondered why he bothered trying to explain anything any more.

He watched the dome awhile but it didn't do anything. He was in the process of deciding to find out whether he could pick up his hallucination where he had left off or would have to start over, when the dome disappeared with another ear-pop and left the original flat floor with a woman lying on it. Not an Earth-type woman, but humanoid and female.

Barton remembered Limila. He had seen her for a number of hours, a long time ago—how long? He had largely forgotten her exact differences from women of Earth. But this woman, coming awake, beginning to sit up and shake her head and look around, had to be of the same race. Yes, the extra fingers and toes. The high forehead, Elizabethan hairline straight across the top of the head above the ears. The breasts set so much lower and wider on the ribcage. Then she opened her mouth and snarled at him, and he saw the many small teeth. There had to be at least forty; Limila had about that many.

Barton prepared to make gestures of friendly welcome; he *felt* friendly and welcoming. In truth he felt friendly and welcoming and lustful. Not excessively lustful, because he had developed a method of self-service sex that involved curling up into a ball so that he figured those lobster bastards couldn't see what he was doing without x-rays. He used it sparingly, but often enough to keep some levels of his mind and his prostate gland in reasonable health. So he was not exactly intent on rape when he extended a hand to help his new roommate up off the floor.

She didn't see it that way. She took the hand, pulled on it and launched herself at him in attack. Barton wasn't ready for her; he had not been conducting any real exercise program during his term in the room. In fact he was more flabby and slothful, he suddenly discovered, than he really cared to be.

The woman clamped more than enough of her many teeth onto the ridge of Barton's jawbone below his right ear. One knee missed smashing his crotch, slipping to the outside of his thigh as he twisted. They fell to the floor, he under her. He caught one wrist and felt safe for a moment until her other hand clawed down his forehead; he felt a finger, its nail, digging into his right eye. He panicked then, and screamed; the eye didn't hurt much, but he could feel blood or something worse running down his cheek. He caught the finger, twisted it and could feel it break, but that wasn't much solace. Then the gravity field hit, heavier than he had ever felt it. His ribs creaked and he blacked out. When he woke, he was alone again.

The bitch had got at his eye, all right. It was mostly healed, which didn't surprise him any more, but there was a wavy line pointing from northwest to southeast in anything he saw with his right eye. A wave of despair rolled over him; he felt crippled, mutilated, as though he'd lost an arm or a leg. Barton didn't have much hope for himself, certainly, but the prospect of a permanent ditch in his vision was more embittering than anything that had happened since his sex had first been turned off.

He couldn't blame the woman too much; he had seen some marks on her that probably would not cause her to view a strange man as a guardian angel. But Barton had the distinct idea that there had to be somebody around who should pay up accounts. He almost got rid of the shock in his corner-sitting hallucinations, but it wouldn't quite go away. After a while he let it alone. Over a time his sight slowly returned to normal, but his feelings didn't.

The second time the dome came, Barton happened to be looking at it. There was the flat floor, and then "pop" there was the dome. About fifty pulse beats later, it disappeared. Barton was hard put to describe in his own mind the female creature on the floor, but by comparing some marks he'd seen the first time, he had to admit it was somewhat the same woman who had clawed his eye.

A few minor alterations had been made. The fingers and toes were shorter and scarred at the ends; each end joint with its claw had been lopped off. Half-healed scars ran down the sides of the head at the temples, just forward of the Queen Elizabeth hairline. Barton knew what this might be, but hoped he was wrong. He wasn't; the woman looked up and gave him a blank childlike stare. Then she smiled, and Barton cursed all the lobsters that ever were. How many teeth had Siewen said—forty? Now, none.

The smiling dull-eyed creature climbed into his lap and hugged him. It took some time before Barton could bring himself to let her kiss him. But she was persistent, and Barton had been alone a very long time.

What was left of the woman had very simple tastes. She loved to eat, off the floor with both hands, which was really the most efficient method. She was quite unhousebroken until the floor conditioned her electrically to use the proper corner most of the time; she cared nothing for cleanliness or appearance.

She was diligently but not urgently horny; after his first lapse Barton fended her off for a time in the interests of what he considered self-respect. But after he once woke to find her straddling him and too late to stop, he gave in and enjoyed it, occasionally. He did keep an eye on the window wall and was prepared to stop at any moment if he saw robed lobsters, but he put out of his mind the possibility that they could watch unseen. After a while he had sex regularly with her, just as though she had been a fully rational intelligent person. After all, she did like it, didn't she?

Sometimes it bothered him that she couldn't talk. Not only his language, but *any* language. He told himself it wasn't his doing, but the telling didn't help much.

He was so unused to paying heed to her bodily functions that he was considerably surprised to realize, eventually, that she had become not merely fat in the gut but alarmingly advanced in pregnancy. Barton simply had not considered the chance of interspecies fertility. She began to have increasing spasms of ill health; Barton's sex life ceased abruptly. He spent much time trying to make signals to the blank wall that had been a window. There were no answers.

Barton sweat up a storm. He knew he couldn't handle what was going to happen in a little while, that he would have been out of his depth delivering a normal easy birth, with full plumbing and antiseptic facilities. He had none of these and the birth was not at all normal, but very difficult. Barton cursed and prayed and got his hands awfully bloody, and the woman-shell was not beyond pain, unfortunately. She screamed and cried as pitifully as though she had had her whole mind with her.

At the last of it, when nothing else could help her, he tried to kill her painlessly in a way the Army had taught him. But the lobsters still knew a trick worth two of that: their gravity gadget. When Barton woke up, it was hard to tell which way he hurt the most. The woman was gone, finally now, and for the last of it he blamed himself.

Barton had given up caring about time passage when the room gave him the second woman. This one looked like Earth ancestry, very young, just past puberty. Like Limila's fellow citizen, she was toothless, temple-scarred and one joint short of nails on fingers and toes. Barton staggered over to a corner and threw up, without regard to where the plumbing was supposed to be.

He couldn't ignore her, though, because she too was strongly sex-oriented and kept trying to get to him whether he was awake or asleep. There was no way to beat that kind of dedication. So he introduced the girl to sexual juxtapositions that could not result in pregnancy, and for quite a long time he thought he had the situation whipped. But one "morning" he woke to find that he couldn't stop the girl from following the example of her predecessor; she had managed to bring him into a "normal" sex act without waking him until the onrush of climax.

Without thought, with only rage, Barton made one move too quickly to be countered. He swung the hard side of his hand and broke the girl's neck. The gravity field hit him then, and he didn't fight it. All he needed was a time to cry for his dead. But when he woke he felt no grief—only emptiness.

They left him alone for a while, until the beginning of what he recognized as language lessons. When the window began showing sets of visual symbols matched with the first sounds he had heard from outside, he knew what they had in mind. He felt, Barton did, that it was a little late for that crap. He already knew all the important things. And it might be advisable to deny the lobsters the insight into his own mind that they might gain by observing his learning processes. Each time the lessons began, he faced the opposite wall. He was pretty deeply into self-hypnosis, and thus fairly successful in ignoring the sounds.

They turned off his sex again. He learned to hallucinate it so well that he didn't really care; in fact, since his mind could experience it more often than his body could, it was in some ways an improvement. More and more he stayed in his own mental world, emerging for feeding and elimination but for very little else.

They worsened the flavor of his food, which took some doing. After the shock of the first taste, he ate it and pretended enjoyment. When they made it completely unpalatable he substituted a hallucinatory taste for the actual one and wondered why he hadn't thought of that answer before. They put stenches in his air also, to no avail and for the same reason. One thing was obvious to Barton: he might have been a slow learner, but the lobsters weren't such great shakes either. He had to hand them one thing, though—at least they were getting his attention, more than he liked.

They played games with the temperature, air pressure and floor gravity. Barton played games right back at them, with his growing abilities of hallucination and self-hypnosis. The only things that really got to him, he noted grimly, were of a type that couldn't possibly gain his cooperation.

The first was dropping the oxygen content of his room; he couldn't fight that, but it rendered him unconscious. The second was electrical shocks from the floor; with some effort he could put them on his "Ignore" circuit but the muscle spasms left him sore. And the third, once only and probably due to a loss of temper by some lobster or other, was floating him in the air on zero gravity and suddenly slamming him to the floor. It broke his right forearm. He healed rapidly, of course, but the break was not set. It left him with a lumpy arm, and painful. Barton wondered how that would work with an exoskeleton. He took up a regular exercise program for the first time, so as not to waste a chance to find out, if he ever got one. After a time his physical condition became surprisingly good, even by his own standards. He decided that the food must have been nutritious even though its natural taste was more rancid than not.

When Barton's self-propelled hallucinations began getting out of hand, he figured they were experimenting with drugs in his food. He knew with certainty that here was something that could take his high ground away from him. He had to change his tactics, so he decided to watch the lessons. The same drugs that cut into his control of his own mind should also distort his responses and thus anything the lobsters could learn from them. So when the window next began to show a language lesson, he sat and watched it. Of course he fiddled in a little hallucinatory content to keep things interesting.

He noted that the impersonal symbol-sound pairings had been replaced by one or more lobsters holding up the symbols and making the sounds, with gestures. He found that he understood a lot of it almost immediately; perhaps some of the earlier material had been getting through on a subliminal basis while he thought he had been ignoring it. Since he did not *want* to learn lobster language he forced himself to ignore as many as possible of the meanings that came intuitively into his mind at each sound-symbol-gesture showing. And after several depictions of a concept that he was fairly sure meant "friendship," he stood up and deliberately pissed on the window. His act brought the lesson to an abrupt end. The lobsters conferred with each other in something resembling a state of excitement; then two converged on the twitchy one Barton had noticed when the creatures had first shown themselves. At least it looked like the same twitchy lobster; there might be more than one. If I were a lobster and had me in a cage, Barton thought, I might feel a little twitchy myself. Then he chalked that thought off to a natural paranoia and watched the outside action more closely.

The three lobsters were coming closer to the window, the twitchy one in the middle, the other two apparently urging it forward. Sure as hell, Barton thought, that one looked different. Not so much like a lobster; the texture was wrong. But the features were about the same, what he could see of them.

Barton had the feeling of almost recognizing the twitchy softer-looking lobster, when it spoke to him. "Barton! For your own good you must—" The lobster face broke into entirely unlobsterlike spasms and the voice went shrill. "No, DON'T! Let them kill you first! I was once—" And the window turned back to gray wall.

Well. The voice had been in English. The sound quality was distorted abominably, but he'd detected only overtones of any "lobster accent." There had been a hint of familiarity to that voice, and so far as he knew, Barton had never been on speaking terms with a lobster. But he had the feeling that there was something he should be remembering.

Then there were new scents in the air and Barton guessed that the lobsters had hit upon breathing-type drugs to bend his mind. Serve the hardshelled bastards right if they killed him first, he thought for a' moment, before he passed out cold.

The problem was that any chemical agent in the food or air that broke Barton's will also dispersed his powers of concentration. After all, those were two looks at the same bag of ego, though Barton had not previously considered the matter in those terms. He had not, he began to realize, considered a lot of things. For one, he hadn't given much thought to why he should be so important to the lobsters, out of the fifty or so people he'd seen in the first cage, maybe two or ten years earlier. It hadn't occurred to him that perhaps the lobsters had stupidly and inefficiently killed most of the rest in their clumsy experimentation, and were getting worried. It seemed a fair guess, though, now that he thought of it.

A different mind than Barton's, he recognized, might have seized upon that possibility and hoped to do some bargaining with it. Barton's mind was stuck on the picture of a mutilated mindless woman forced to die in horrible pain. It was not exactly revenge that held his thinking; it was more on the order of Corrective Annihilation . . . something like a Roman galley slave with a fixation on the extermination of the Caesars. The idea amused him a little, but not much. Idly he wondered what had become of the easygoing fellow he used to be, and decided that that man had died with the Tilaran woman.

Now, though, he thought he knew his one possible chance for escape. He'd figured it out; the logic was flawless. The only problem was that he had no idea whether he could really do it or not.

For a time, then, Barton played an intense and deadly game with the language lessons, a game his would-be teachers could not be equipped to recognize. He would register understanding of one symbol, no comprehension of the next, confusion about another, in a calculated fashion. Today's knowledge was tomorrow's incomprehension, he pretended. His idea was to drive the lobsters as nuts as he suspected *he* was becoming.

It worked for longer than he had expected. The lobsters took long pauses during the lesson sessions, conferred in their tinny little voices, and became so agitated as to reach under their robes and apparently scratch. Barton didn't see how a lobster could get much of a kick out of scratching itself.

The twitchy one didn't show up again in the window. That figured.

During the between-lessons periods Barton had been pushing himself as hard and as far as he could manage it, along the lines of heavy self-hypnosis. The drugs were out of his food and air now that he was "cooperating" with the lessons, and he worked that breathing spell for all it was worth. Because there wouldn't be more than one chance, and while that one might not be worth the effort, what *else* could he do?

When the creatures in the window got tired of his lack of progress and began jarring him again with floor shocks, Barton knew he had to try it. He gave them a little jelly for their bread with his responses to the remainder of that lesson. When the window turned back into gray wall he curled up in the middle of the floor, well away from the latrine and feeding areas, and began willing himself as close to death as he might possibly get back from, and perhaps a little further. Besides hallucination and self-hypnosis and faking, he threw in considerably more true death wish than he would have done if he were still capable of giving a real damn. He knew what he was doing, but it didn't frighten him. The floor would not allow passage of a living organism; therefore Barton had to be effectively dead. That was how he had figured it,

what he was betting on. There was no other chance for
Barton, none at all.

The sensation of interpenetrating the floor was disturb-
ing beyond anything he could have imagined; he hadn't
expected to be able to feel anything. But his will held;
he gave no betraying heartbeat. Some ghost at the back
of his mind tried to guess how many pounds of his own
excrement he was finally following, but the estimate was
impossible. He didn't know how many years it had been,
let alone his average excretion.

The sudden drop through the air and subsequent impact jarred him. He saw through slit-tight eyelids that
he was on the floor of a corridor. At least he had lucked
out and missed the plumbing. Only one robed lobster was
in sight. It approached, bent over him and reached . . .

In two breaths Barton was alive again. He caught a
bruise and a laceration across the face before he had the
chance to prove his theory that with the proper leverage,
the limbs of an exoskeleton shatter beautifully. When the
lobster began to make its characteristic noises, Barton
kicked the back of its skull in, holding it against the
floor and stomping again and again with his bare heel
until the thing crumpled.

At that point, like it or not, he had to stop and take
stock. His flirtation with near-death had left him weak,
and his soul was equally shaken. Barton's vision was flickering around the edges; he waited until it settled down.
Then he stripped the robe from the lobster-creature and
looked at the latter with great care.. It wasn't all that
impressive, he decided.

All right. The thing was outer-shelled for the most
part, but not boilerplate with joints. Instead, the surface
went gradually from hardshell to gristle where it needed
to bend. The shapes of limb segments were not unlike
the endoskeletal human, but of course rigid on the outside. The soles of the feet and palms of hands were
the softest and most padded parts of the body. Up the
center of the abdomen ran a hand's-width pattern of
dots, some concave and some convex. The crotch was devoid of anything Barton might have expected; it was like
a branching tree.

Barton didn't take long, seeing what there was to see; it took him longer to decide what to do. Not so very long, though. He searched the robe, found a small cutting implement. He carved a great part of the shell off the front and top of the creature's head, pissed in it to wash out most of the brownish blood, and wiped the thing dry with the tail of the robe. Then he put it on his own head. The eyeholes didn't quite fit, so he took it off and gouged them a little larger. He didn't look at what still lay on the floor. Not yet.

Everything inside him said to put on the robe and hood and move out of there, but Barton knew that first he needed something more on his side. He had no real weapon except his ability to break exoskeletal arms and legs, which did not seem quite enough. So, messy hands or not, he took his dead lobster apart rather thoroughly. He didn't even throw up.

He learned that the creature's main nerve trunks were ventral rather than dorsal, and down its middle found the bonus of a fine sword-shaped "bone" that needed only some lobster foot-cartilage to serve as hilt-wrapping.

Barton decided that time was running out. There was no way to hide his gutted lobster in the narrow corridor, so he left it. He chose his direction simply: the way he could step least in the juices of the corpse. He kept his "sword" and the other cutting tool under his borrowed robe, out of sight.

When Barton met a pair of real live lobsters face to face in one of the corridors, he came close to losing his toilet training. He had no idea what to do. He knew that no one person can stand off an enemy population in its home territory. So he tried to pretend to be a lobster who didn't want to talk to anybody, and it worked. After that experience he merely kept moving and hoped that nobody would cross him. Nobody did; Barton decided that maybe lobsters were too mean even for other lobsters.

After a time, Barton came to the top of an up-ramp and saw the sky. Now he knew that he had been kept underground, for however long it had been. He set out walking, paying no more attention than he could help to the lapse of time since he had last had food or drink.

The sky was spectacular, but Barton couldn't be

bothered. There were stars in the daytime, for instance. Barton couldn't have cared less. He needed a place to sleep. He found a clump of odd-looking brush and crawled into it, hungry and thirsty and cold.

The lobster that found Barton and poked him with a stick to wake him was a very unlucky lobster. Barton's sword was entangled in his robe, so he bashed its head in with a fist-sized rock. Then, his hunger and weakness overcoming any remaining scruples, he ate the tender flesh of its forearm, raw. It was something like crab meat, and the best-tasting food he'd had since they caught him. He decided he was beginning to develop a taste for the place. He also decided that he scared himself.

Barton was beginning to believe that he was invincible. When he didn't meet any more lobsters, he was sure of it. He blanked out all idea of how weak and vulnerable he really was, because his mind didn't want to work along those lines. He accepted the knowledge that his hallucinations were no longer entirely separate from his objective experiences, and hadn't been since he didn't know when. There was something about a woman . . .

While he was gnawing at the last of a lobsterish forearm, Barton stumbled onto the outskirts of a field scattered with odd-looking vehicles, dully metallic in hue. Anyone with half sense had to know that a saucerlike object in such a place would be a spaceship, so Barton sprinted for a saucer.

It was bigger than it had looked from a distance, about forty feet in diameter. The bottom surface curved upward; the outer edge was inches higher than he could reach and offered no handhold to jump for. He walked around it, looking for access and finding none. Dammit, there had to be a way into the thing! He stood for a moment, baffled, then began a second and slower circuit, inspecting the surface above him inch by inch.

Ahead, out of sight around the curve of metal, Barton heard a sound of machinery in motion. Carefully he disengaged his bone sword from the robe and advanced, to see a curved ramp descending from an area about midway between edge and center of the saucer shape. He scuttled forward, to be under and behind it as it touched ground. Then he waited. Somebody certainly was in no hurry. His sword hand was sweaty; he wiped it on his robe and discarded his lobster-mask for better vision.

When Barton heard footsteps above he peeked around the edge of the ramp. One robed lobster was descending. Barton waited to see if more would come· or if this one would look back and say anything to others in the vehicle. Neither happened; there was only one lobster.

As it stepped off the ramp, the mechanism began to rise, slowly. Barton took three steps forward and swung his sword to belt the lobster across the side of the head as hard as he could. It went down but didn't stay down; it came up facing Barton. Holding the sword hilt in both hands, he lunged to the midsection with his full weight. The thrust bounced off but the creature dropped, holding itself and breathing in ragged gulps. Out of breath himself, Barton let go the sword, turned and jumped to grab the end of the ramp.

The gap was within inches of closing; the thought flashed through his mind that he could lose some fingers. But with his weight on the ramp, it sank again. He didn't wait; as soon as there was clearance he scrambled on and clambered up as fast as he could manage.

At the top was a door. Barton turned its handle and pushed the door open, wishing he hadn't had to leave the sword behind. But he found only an empty corridor. A glance below showed that the lobster wasn't having much luck getting up, so Barton didn't wait to see the ramp all the way closed. He found the way to secure the door from inside, and settled for that.

There were a lot of doors, and presumably compartments behind them. Barton ignored these and stayed on the main corridor. A little later, in a closed windowless room that he also locked from inside, he looked at the control assembly and wondered if it made *any* sense.

There had to be a way to find out, if he could think of it. For starters, there was a projecting lever that swung smoothly in every direction, to no effect. And another that moved only up and down, but nothing happened there either. And a neat rectangle of what seemed to be toggle switches, with one larger turquoise-handled one in the center. Starting at top left and working to the right, like reading an English-language book, Barton gingerly flipped each of the smaller toggle switches up and immediately back down, to see if by momentary activation he could get some clues without necessarily killing himself.

Nothing happened. OK, Barton said to Barton. The swivel bar has to steer this thing, and the up-and-downer has to be the go pedal. Or else I am already dead and just don't know it yet. And these other flips are auxiliary controls. So the big blue devil in the middle has to be where the action starts.

Checking to see that all the toggles were back where he'd started, and the two levers also as near to neutral as he could tell, he flipped the turquoise switch. There came a heavy pervasive hum all around him, then a thin screaming from somewhere else in the place. The scream wasn't steady like the hum; without thinking, Barton left the controls and went looking for it, on the run.

It was a smaller-than-average lobster, about three-quarter scale. Barton caught it trying to unlock the door to outside. Every impulse shrieked at him to kill it, but even now he had a soft spot for small, presumably young creatures, so he tried to subdue it instead. Paradoxically, his weakness prevented him from doing so without injuring it—in the struggle he accidentally broke one of its arms. He dragged it back to the control area, and using its own robes, tied it down into a seat. Still it screamed.

The high piercing sound didn't help Barton's concentration. His sight was flickering again, like an out-of-tune TV set with the pictures jiggling to the peaks of the sound track. His ears filled the silences with a dull ringing and once a voice spoke in his head: "Give it up, Barton. You lost." When the control panel began to change into a gray wall he fought himself back from past the brink of panic and proceeded to reason with the small screaming lobster in the only way he could manage.

He persuaded it to stop screaming, and then to stop a kind of whimpering, by giving it a full open-hand slap across the eyes every time it made a noise. After a while it got the point. Barton was glad, because his hand was getting as sore as his sensibilities. So was his throat; he had accompanied every slap with a shout. He was parched thirsty.

His spaceship was still humming. Barton tried his tentative steering and throttle levers but nothing happened. Well, then; back to the rectangle of toggles.

The first few, as he flipped them quickly on and off, did nothing spectacular. The one at the right end of the top row made the whole machine push up at him gently. He flipped it full on, then, and realized the thing had to be airborne. Flying by the seat of his pants, he worked his self-designated throttle and steering levers gingerly, and found that indeed they gave the feelings of acceleration and turning that he had expected. So he went straight up, the best way he knew to keep from hitting anything while he figured things better.

The only trouble was, he still couldn't see out. Also the little lobster was keening again, and he couldn't spare a hand to slap it.

Suddenly Barton was standing under a great golden dome, with deep tones of organ music reverberating around him. He shook his head; this was no time to play around with hallucinations, even pleasant ones. It was hard to get back. He had spent a lot of time perfecting that mental escape from the lobsters' cage, he was beat all out of shape, and the miniature Demu's noise was disrupting his thought patterns badly.

But he made it, and instead of slapping his small lobster to shut it up he took a deep breath, bracing himself, and hit them both with a heavy-G vertical swerve. It did the job; he had silence. Then he went back to the methodical quick testing of the bank of switches.

He was a long time finding the one that gave him an outside view, and somewhat longer in learning that the toggle switches also twisted to give fine controls such as focus or magnification. It was then that he found he hadn't captured a spaceship after all.

It was nothing but some kind of goddamned air car. There were quite a few more of the same, hanging with him and surrounding him. Barton didn't quite panic, but he did try to make a run for it. It didn't work; they stayed right with him. His mind had not quite decided to run away from home and leave him to manage by himself when he noticed that neither his nor the other airborne vehicles could approach each other too closely; some invisible cushion kept them apart. Barton the ex-physicist thought briefly on the possible ways of obtaining such an effect; then Barton the escaped caged animal took over, wanting only to escape what came at him, or smash it if necessary. He explained the position to his captive lobster several times, but it did not answer, having learned that noise would cause it to be hit, by Barton. It did get up the nerve to say "Whnee," quietly. Barton took this well; he smiled and did not slap the smallish lobster. The exchange might eventually have developed into the first conversation between Barton and a Demu, if he had had the time for it. But of course he didn't.

Barton, though, was only stretched out of shape, not out of commission. He went back to testing the switches that he'd merely flicked before to see that they wouldn't kill him; now he left each one on long enough to see what it controlled. So sooner or later he had to turn on the visual and voice intercom, through which the opposition appeared to have been trying to reach him for quite some time. It was the third switch from the right in the fourth row from the top.

The big lobster in the foreground of the viewscreen broke into excited gestures and loud shrill sounds, so Barton knew the view was two-way. The smaller lobster beside him shrilled back in answer. It was all too loud and too fast for him to follow, but finally it struck him that they were exchanging communication he didn't understand.

He could *not* allow them to talk over his head. That way led back to the cage. Bracing himself so as not to move the controls accidentally, Barton belted the small lobster across the eyes as hard as he could, backhand. It felt like hitting a rock; he hoped he hadn't broken his hand. The creature slumped limply; brownish fluid dripped from one nostril-hole and a corner of its mouth. Barton felt remorse, but only briefly: he didn't have time for it.

The big one on the screen was yammering again; Barton couldn't follow the text. He shook his head impatiently. He knew it was his own stupid fault for not going along better with the language lessons, but he didn't feel like admitting any blame. "You want to talk with ME, you lobster-shelled bastard, you talk MY language!" he shouted. "TALK ENGLISH, or go to hell!"

He repeated this with variations while with half his mind he jockeyed the air car against the attempts of his escort to herd him in the direction of their choice. The other air cars surrounded him and tried to mass their pressure shields to move Barton the way they wanted him to go, but there weren't enough to hold him and push him at the same time. And he was feeling just stubborn enough to fight anything they wanted him to do: anything at all. Hallucinations nibbled at him, but now he decided they must be effects of the Demu unconsciousness weapon, leaking past the air car's shields. The hypothesis, true or not, made it surprisingly easier to fight the phantoms off. So with something like enjoyment he used his considerable kinesthetic skills to thwart their efforts to herd him. The upshot was that the dozen or so air cars danced around much the same area for quite a while before the next development on the viewscreen. Which was that it spoke his name.

"Barton!" it said. "Thish ish Shiewen. You musht lishen to me!" On the screen was what Barton had come to think of as the twitchy lobster, the one that didn't look quite like the rest. It sounded like a voice he knew, and now he remembered Doktor Siewen. But why would Siewen sound like a comic drunk act?

Barton put the odd pronunciation to the back of his mind and concentrated on the meaning. "Doctor Siewen? I don't believe it. Throw that damn hood back and let me see you." It seemed strange to be *talking* with anyone, anyone at all.

As the hands came up and the hood went back, Barton heard a ghost voice: Doktor Siewen's. "They catch people and turn them into Demu."

They sure as hell did. Without the hair and ears and nose and eyebrows, with the serrated lips over toothless gums and a shortened stumpy tongue, the thing on the screen didn't look much like Siewen except for the chin and cheekbones. But the skull and neck were human-shaped, not lobsterish. The eyelids looked a little odd; Barton decided they'd been trimmed back to get rid of the eyelashes. And a long-forgotten memory reminded him that the sounds of *s* and *z* cannot be made without touching the tongue to teeth or gums at the front of the mouth; otherwise the result is *sh* and *zh*. He put that answer in cold storage, too, trying to absorb the shock.

It wasn't that the creature on the screen was so horrible in itself; when you've seen one lobster you've seen them all. The obscenity was in knowing what it had been before the Demu had set to work. Barton had thought he hated the lobsters already; he found he hadn't even begun.

"All right; it's you, I guess," he said. "I'm listening; go ahead." Idly he noticed the hands with three fingers and no nails; the jog at the wristline showed that the little finger had been stripped away, all along the palm. He bet himself a few dead lobsters on the condition of Siewen's feet, then shook his head and listened.

"Barton, you musht come back." Barton's mind, back where he wasn't paying too much attention to it, was irritated by the distraction of the distorted sibilants and decided to ignore them. "The young Demu you have is the egg-child of the Director of this research station. Shut off your shield; it is two up and three over from bottom left of your switch panel. The Director offers you full Demu citizen rights."

Barton chuckled; sometimes you draw a good card. "Well now, is that *right?*" Not waiting for an answer because he didn't need one, he went on: "Forget what the Director wants. Forget what the Director offers. If the Director wants his gimpy-arm egg-child back in mostly one piece, the important thing is what *I* want. And for starters, I don't need any company around here. Get this bunch of sheepdogs off my back; I won't talk any more until you do. And get that damned sleep-gadget off my mind, too. I'll wait." By *God*, but it was good to be able to talk back for a change, to have a little bit of personal say-so. He waited, not too impatiently.

Soon the surrounding air cars grouped to his right and departed. The twitchy lobster who had been Doktor Siewen came back to the screen. Barton spoke first.

"Now I want information. Lots of it. How much fuel time do I have in this kite? And look, Siewen, or whatever you are by now—tell him, don't anybody try to shit me about anything. Because, anybody gets tricky, nobody can stop me from using this bucket to kill myself. They know damn well I've been trying to do that for a long time. And there goes the Director's egg-child, whatever that means, right down the spout along with me. You got that straight?"

Siewen nodded, scuttled back to exchange shrill communications with the Director.

You may be the King of the Lobsters, thought Barton, but to me you're just one damned big overgrown crawdad!

Siewen came back to face Barton. "It is not fuel, your problem," he said. "Thirst and hunger, yes. You have no food or water, Barton. You must come in; I give you directions. Yes?"

Barton looked at the small comatose lobster beside him, and snorted. After all this time, these creatures still didn't realize what they had on their hands, what they had made of him.

For one thing, they were still trying to lie. Rummaging under his seat, he had found a container of liquid: about two quarts and nearly full. It smelled as if it could be lobster piss and maybe it was, but probably it wouldn't kill him. No point in telling everything he knew, though, Barton thought.

"Where are you, Siewen? I don't mean the location, but what kind of place?"

"It is Director's office, of the research station. Also control area for spaceship landing place just alongside. You can get here easily. Location device, bottom left switch, homes on signal beacon here. Small instrument." Siewen pointed; the thing looked like a portable radio. "Just watch on screen."

"Sure. Are there spaceships there?"

"Yes, several. Different sizes."

Barton told himself to be very, very cautious. "Siewen, has the Director ever been to Earth? Our Earth?"

"Oh yes," Siewen responded. "He was in charge of navigation on expedition picking ourselves up. But first time he or this group ever see humans or Tilari, any of our type humanoid. Some mistakes they made." You can say *that* again, Barton thought. But now he needed more facts, in a hurry.

"What's the smallest ship available that could get from

here to Earth? How many does it take to handle such a ship? TELL THEM NOT TO LIE TO ME!"

"There is no cause to lie," Siewen said calmly. "A ship to carry eight is here; it could go twice to Earth and back; one can control it. But you are not to go to Earth, Barton. You are to come here and become a citizen of the Demu. Out of the mercy of the Director and his concern for his egg-child."

Deep in his throat Barton growled, not quite audibly. "We'll see," he said. "Take that robe off, Siewen."

"What? Why?"

"Just do it."

He had known all along, Barton thought wearily. He glanced perfunctorily at the feet, long enough to confirm that the little toes had been cut away back through the metatarsals to the heels, and that the toenails were missing. The obliteration of body hair and nipples and navel was no shock, nor was the Demu pattern of abdominal dots. And of course the crotch was like that of a tree, or a lobster.

Siewen must have noticed Barton's gaze; one hand tentatively reached for that juncture, then drew back. "You don't understand," Siewen said. "They didn't know. I said, it was first time this group had to do with humans. Only with other races, not like us. They didn't *know*."

"Sure not," said Barton.

"I don't really mind so, any more," Siewen said hurriedly, "and they don't do that way now. They learned, some from observing you, Barton. Now they retain function and only minimize protrusion. There is one here, done so. I must show."

"Later!" Barton ground out. He didn't want to see any more examples of Demu surgical artistry for a while; his will to live was shaken enough, as it was. "Just tell me one thing, will you? *Why* do they do these things?"

"Hard to understand, for us. But Demu are old race, very old. And for long long time they know of no others, intelligent. They have deep belief, almost instinct, that Demu are the only true *people*. That all others are only animals."

"Well, haven't they learned better than that by *now*? And what does that have to do with—your facelift, and everything?"

"When they meet long ago a race, animals they think, who learn Demu language, it is great shock. Animals being people when only Demu are people. Demu cannot accept. So they—this is only guess by me, you understand, but I think it is very good guess—so they when any animal learns Demu language, make it Demu, best they can. As with me and others. They make mistakes; many die. I am lucky." Barton thought that was a matter of opinion. He didn't bother to say so.

He was still digesting what he had heard when Siewen's voice reminded him that this was no time for philosophizing. He had things to do, fast, before the opposition caught its balance. He couldn't afford to get off the main point.

"Barton!" Siewen began. "You must—"

"LATER! Siewen, get your Director up front with you and translate for us. I'm in a hurry; tell him that; don't either of you try to mess around with me. Now MOVE!"

Barton told them exactly what he wanted. They didn't believe him at first, and he supposed they would have laughed if a lobster knew how to laugh. But he persisted, figuring that he had an ace in the hole.

"Barton," said Siewen, "you are speaking useless. The Director will not give you a spaceship to go to Earth. No one can command the Demu."

"Does the Director want his egg-child back alive, or doesn't he?"

"Wants back, yes," Siewen acknowledged. "But at your price, no. Demu have died before and will die again." I'll drink to that, thought Barton. "Safe return of egg-child buys you life and citizenship among the Demu. No more. I do not want to tell what will be done if you are taken alive and egg-child dead. Now see reason, Barton. You have tried well. You are admired for it, even. But now it is finish. You must come here and accept Director's terms."

"Want to bet?" thought Barton. But he said, "Tell me one more thing, Siewen. Can the Demu regrow lost limbs? Like the lobsters back home?"

"No," said Siewen. "Why ask that?"

"Just curious." Barton paused for a moment, thinking it out. "Siewen, tell the Director that I am getting very hungry." There was a muffled conference on the screen.

"The Director says come here and be fed," Siewen announced. Barton grinned.

"I don't have to," he said softly. "Let me tell you about the last meal I had."

He told them, and the funny part was that Siewen seemed every bit as shocked as the Director. Barton let them chew on the idea a minute before he threw the bomb.

"OK, Siewen, here's how it works. Tell the Director and tell it straight. Either I get the ship to go home in, instructions and all, and the deal gets started right away, or else I have lunch now." He thought about it. "Considering everything, I don't feel especially sadistic. So first I'll just eat the arm I've already broken. I'll leave the screen off, so the Director doesn't have to watch."

Barton hadn't thought a Demu-lobster could get as loud as the Director did then. Eventually Siewen got the floor. It seemed Barton had won his point; he had a good healthy ship for himself. Sure, Mike, thought Barton; just watch out for the curve balls.

Well, he'd known there had to be a handle somewhere in the mess; luckily he'd found it. It had been a one-shot bluff, a game of *schrecklicheit*—because it would have done him no good to carry it out, even if he could have brought himself to do so. But what the Director didn't know wouldn't hurt Barton.

His mind was getting hazy again, ghost-hallucinations flickering around the outskirts. Toothlessly, the Tilari woman was telling him that they were expecting a little bundle from Heaven. He shook his head and tried to concentrate on the essentials.

"OK, Siewen," he said, "I don't need any coordinates to get to you, if I understand this location-blip thing on the screen." Siewen nodded. "Here's what happens," Barton continued. "You and the Director get down by the ship—my ship. Bring your locator gadget with you so I don't have to mess around looking for you when I get there. Everybody else stays away. Any last-minute tricks, I cut the shield and ram us all dead. You got that? Any questions?"

There were several, but Barton simply said "NO" to most of them without paying much attention. He knew what he wanted. There was no point in arguing.

Then Siewen, at the Director's prompting, insisted Barton should see and talk with some other newly made citizens of the Demu, before doing anything so drastic as what he was planning. "The hell with that," said Barton. "Later. Just you two. Nobody else."

It was about an hour that Barton's air car took, cruising to its destination. He saw no signs of habitation; possibly the research station was the only Demu installation on the planet. The little lobster was conscious again and whimpered occasionally, but it looked so apologetic that Barton didn't feel like hitting it, even to maintain the precedent of silence. Anyway, the small sounds weren't joggling his mind as the screaming had done. He sipped on the foul-tasting water and decided it wasn't lobster piss after all, since his small lobster made begging motions toward it, and drank some when he relented and made the offer. Then it opened its mouth and lifted its short tongue. Barton had no idea what the gesture meant, but the creature rewarded his generosity with silence. It was a good trade.

The spaceport, when he reached it, didn't look like much. There were three really big ships, two medium and one small. Upright torpedo shapes, not saucers. The big ones would be the meat wagons, he thought. They had an air of neglect about them.

He set the car to hover a little above and to one side of the small ship, facing a delegation of robed figures at fairly close range. He cranked up magnification on the direct-view display screen, and saw that there were four of them.

"What the hell you think you're doing?" Barton said. "I said *nobody else.*"

Siewen shrugged and spread his arms apologetically. "You must see other new Demu citizens," he said. "You said later, but only chance is now. You must know. With me there were mistakes, yes. But these are functional breeders and Demu citizens. As millions of Earth humans will become, and all eventually, when the Demu have arranged. But see—! You will not forget Limila; the other is of Earth." Siewen gestured.

The two figures slipped off their hoods and robes. Barton took for granted the hairless earless noseless heads with serrated lips hiding toothless mouths with shortened tongues. (But oh! the lost lovely curve of Limila's lips!) He didn't expect to see breasts set low on Limila's ribcage, and sure enough, there weren't any. The lobsters scrubbed clean, singlemindedly. Siewen had said that the smooth treelike look of her, where Barton was looking now, still concealed true function: even so, it was one more coal on the fire in Barton's heart and mind.

Then there was the man, an Earthman if Siewen had that part right. Siewen had certainly told truth that the Demu had "minimized protrusion" in the genital area; whether or not the Demu citizen on the screen "retained function" was of only academic interest to Barton. He was trying very hard not to throw up. It's like the old joke about the man who went into the barbershop, he thought. "Bob Peters here?" "No, just shave-and-a-haircut."

"Siewen!" he shouted. "I've changed my mind."

"You come now and become Demu citizen?"

"Like bloody hell I do!" Barton, bursting with frustration and hatred, took especial pains not to turn and kill the small lobster beside him. Hell, it probably hadn't even carved up its first human yet.

"Then what is it you mean?" said Siewen.

"I mean we all go on the ship," Barton said. "The two of us here and the four of you there. All together we go in; don't move yet, any of you, or I crash the lot of us."

There was a conference down below. "Not possible," said Siewen. "The Director does not agree."

"In that case," said Barton, "I think it's time I had some lunch. I've changed my mind; I'll leave the screen on so that the Director can observe. I always did like crab salad." And he reached for the dangling broken arm of the small quiet lobster, the Director's egg-child.

Not too much later the Demu spacecraft lifted off, carrying six assorted entities with very little rapport.

The ship's basic control system was roughly the same as the air car's, though with many more control switches. For the moment, all Barton needed was power, navigation and an outside view. He'd worry about the rest of it later, when he had to.

Siewen assured Barton that the Director had given him the correct course toward the region of Earth, and had agreed there would be no pursuit. Barton assured Siewen that the Director damn well better had, if the Director wanted Barton to watch his diet.

A tense truce prevailed, largely because of Barton's policy that he would not put up with the company of fully functional Demu. He had broken one of the Director's arms the moment they were sealed inside the ship, when that worthy had tried to make use of a concealed weapon. Then after a moment's thought, he broke the other one. Subtler methods might have done the job, but Barton had found something that worked, so he stayed with it. He had trouble thinking outside the narrow boundaries of his main goal: freedom. The Director treated Barton with considerable respect, and was fed at intervals by his egg-child, one-handedly.

Barton set and splinted the broken limbs, which was more than the Demu had bothered to do for him in like case. His own forearm still had a permanent jog to it and hurt more often than it didn't.

That wasn't all the hurt in Barton. Limila remembered him; the Demu hadn't done anything to her mind, that he could detect. He realized, though, that he wasn't much of a judge of minds. Including his own.

She came to him, in the control area which he never left unguarded; when he slept, he sealed it off from the rest of the ship. She told him, in her *sh-zh* lobster accent, that she wanted love with him. She parted her maimed lips and showed the Demu-shortened tongue lifted in what he now knew to be the Demu smile. With the forty teeth gone he could see it quite clearly.

The trouble was that the Demu-Limila still had Limila's shape of skull and chin and cheekbones. The quicksilver-colored huge-irised eyes were as deep as ever, though their shape was subtly marred by the slight cropping of the eyelids. Her arms and legs were graceful if Barton avoided seeing the hands and feet, and aside from breasts and navel and external genitals, the Demu had not altered her superb lithe torso.

Barton closed his eyes to shut out the sight of the Demu-denuded face and head, put his cheek against Limila's and tried to make love with her. It might have worked if he hadn't noticed the ear that should have been against his nose and wasn't. So instead he failed; he failed her. He was crying when he gently put her out of the control area and relocked it, and for a long time after.

Then he went into the main passenger compartment to see if he could keep from killing the Director and his egg-child out of hand; for the moment, he succeeded. It was a success that helped Barton's dwindling self-confidence. He had all he could do to keep himself under control, let alone keeping the ship on course or his fellow-voyagers in hand.

For one thing he was continually bone-tired. The pseudo-death experience had taken more out of him than he'd realized at first. Followed by a period of hectic activity and nervous tension, and now the need for near-constant alertness, it still dragged him down; recovery was so slow as to be indetectable.

His condition made him easy prey to mental lapses. He became accustomed to waking, as often as not, to find himself apparently back in his cage; each time it took minutes to fight his way back to reality. More frightening were occasional hallucinatory lapses in the presence of others: once he found himself on the verge of defending his Ph.D. Orals presentation to the professor who had washed him out, before he realized that the prof couldn't possibly be there; it was the Director who sat before him.

Every sight of Limila burned more deeply into him than the last, into a place where gentleness had once lived. Where now grew something else—something that frightened him.

He didn't let the others see his difficulties any more than he could help, and they were too afraid of him to try to take advantage of his lapses. They were not wrong; Barton was walking death and knew it; he had been for longer than he liked to admit. He kept to himself as much as possible, consonant with the need to keep tabs on his passengers.

Once he looked into a mirror and found he didn't recognize himself. He had no idea how long it had been since he might have been able to do so. He looked at the face in the mirror and decided he didn't like it. But then it wasn't really his own work, he realized when he stopped to think about it. The thought made him feel a little better, but not much.

So it was a long tired haul. The "trip out," as Barton thought of it, must have been either on a faster ship or with a lot of induced hibernation; he had no way of knowing which, if either, was the correct guess.

Limila came to him again, wanting his love. He tried to turn her away; she didn't want to go. "Barton," she said, clinging to him desperately, "I am still Limila. They do all this to me, yes"—she stepped back and gestured at her head, at her body—"but inside I am still ME. I AM!" His eyes blurred with tears, losing the fine outline of skull and cheekbones, of neck and shoulders as she stood before him. Seeing, then, only the lobsterish lack of features, it was easier for him to keep shaking his head speechlessly and back her firmly out the door, locking it after her with a vicious yank that nearly broke the lever.

The next time he saw her she was slumped in a corner looking at the floor. He didn't disturb her trance, but it disturbed *him* a lot.

Hallucinating was a dangerous game to play, for him, now; he knew that. But he thought it might be a solution, with Limila. He invited her into the control area, looked at her and deliberately tried to substitute in his mind her natural appearance.

It worked, and for a few moments he thought it was *really* going to work. But his mind-picture of unmaimed-Limila shifted and distorted. Against all the force he could bring, it changed into the other Tilaran woman, the one with no nail-joints, the blank stare and the scars at the temples. It writhed and screamed, dying again. Barton screamed too, but he didn't hear most of it. When he fought his way back to reality, the sight of the lobster-faced Limila seemed almost beautiful. But only almost. He could not love it, would never be able to do that.

Limila crouched against the door, terrified. "You must think I'm crazy," Barton said. "I'm sorry. I thought I could fool myself, pretend you were unchanged. It—it didn't work out quite that way. I saw something worse, instead." He knew he couldn't explain further, and said only, "I'm sorry, Limila."

She went away of her own accord, looking back fearfully.

Barton tried to pair her off with the Demu-ized Earthmale who supposedly "retained function." That one was a real enigma; he wouldn't speak to Barton, or to anyone at all except in Demu. Barton couldn't discover his name or anything else about him, except that apparently he had become Demu wholeheartedly in spirit as well as in guise. Barton decided that when it came down to cases he had more respect for Doktor Siewen. Which wasn't saying much.

At any rate the pseudo-Demu wanted nothing to do with Limila, nor she with him. Barton asked Limila about the matter but wasn't sure whether he misunderstood the answer or simply didn't believe it. "He say," Limila told Barton, "it not Demu breeding season now." She gave Barton the view of uplifted-tongue, the Demu smile. "The Tilari do not wait on season, nor you, I think." But she had smiled like a Demu. Of course, Barton reflected, locking himself alone into the control area, it was the only way they had left her to smile. Well, there wasn't any answer; maybe there never had been. Or not lately.

Barton now avoided Limila almost entirely. It was the only thing he could do for either of them. The next time the functional Demu-Earthmale got in his way, Barton without warning knocked him square on his back against the opposite bulkhead and was happily beginning to kick him to death before Limila tried to push between them, shrilling, "NO, NO! WHY? WHY?" Barton had no answer, shrugged and moved away, marveling at his ability to leave the two Demu alive as long as he had.

Actually, not noticing the change much, Barton had become rather fond of the Director's small egg-child. Without knowing its name, or being able to pronounce it, probably, Barton thought of it as female. He called it "Whnee," after the sound of its rather plaintive little cries when uncertain what was wanted of it. It tried to be helpful with the ship's few chores, and Barton came to think of it as a nice-enough kid; too bad she came from such a rotten family. Occasionally it would make the Demu lifted-tongue smile at him, and oddly he found the gesture not at all repulsive, but rather appealing.

Siewen was no trouble; he was only a shell, not a person. He reflected the thought or policy of the One in Charge; once that had been the Director, now it was Barton. Any authority was good enough for that which had once been Doktor Siewen.

The Director was no problem either. Barton simply didn't bother to take the splint-harnesses off his arms, even when they had probably healed. The other Demu-human tried to unstrap the Director once, but Barton caught him and so reacted that neither Whosits nor anyone else tried it again. It took another set of splints; Barton guessed he was in a rut.

But what the hell; it worked, which was more than Barton could say for much of anything else he'd tried lately. The only late effort he liked much was his clothes. He'd hated the Demu robes, which all the others still wore. He had essayed nudity but found it too reminiscent of his captivity. Eventually he had ripped a robe into two pieces: one made a loincloth and the other a short cape that left his arms free. Barton didn't care what it looked like; it was comfortable. He could use all the comfort he could get.

Finally the ship approached Earth's solar system. Barton was going home. Not really, of course. There was nothing for him there. He knew he'd be lucky to get a hearing before being locked up as a public menace. But he had to take the risk, because it was everybody's chance, maybe the only one Earth would ever get. He wasn't looking for a return to normal life. That wasn't in the cards; he'd been playing too long with a 38-card deck. But there was one thing, for sure.

Barton had survived; maybe Earth could survive. He had to give it the chance to try. He was bringing home a fair sample of what Earth was up against: the lobsters, their ship and some of their other works.

The lobsters would be confined and studied; Barton smiled grimly at that prospect. He wondered how long it would take them to get used to the fact that on Earth it's messy to piss on the floor. He might go to see the little one sometimes if anyone would let him; they could say "Whnee" to each other and maybe now and then she'd raise her tongue in the Demu smile.

He couldn't bring himself to worry about what might

become of Siewen or Whosits; he had enough worry on his own account. But he hoped someone—someone more capable than he—would take care of Limila. All Barton could do was try to take care of Earth, and maybe of Barton with luck.

The ship could help a lot. It and its weapons would be analyzed and copied, maybe even improved. Human science had been moving fast, the last Barton had heard; no telling how much further it had gone.

Most important, though, was showing Earth what the well-barbered humanoid wouldn't be wearing next season if the Demu had their way, as modeled by Siewen and Limila and Whosits. Barton thought he knew how the people of Earth would react.

They wouldn't like it any better than he did. They might decide to teach the Demu what it meant, to cage a man.

PART **II:**

Humpty Dumpty

Barton approached Earth like a boy asking a girl for his first dance. He was dubious of his welcome, both in space and on the ground. Stalling, he took a course that kept the moon between his ship and his destination, while he tried to think his way through the situation.

The alien ship and its occupants were bound to be something of a surprise to the home folks, and it would take time for Barton to get his story across straight. He was braced for that necessity.

What the locals would make of his companions was something else again. It would require a sharp observer, he thought, to tell them apart at first: the Demu, God rot their hypothetical souls, were remorselessly thorough in enforcing conformity of appearance. Barton was hit by a surge of belated relief: maybe he looked like the wrath of God and fresh out of thunderbolts, but at least he still carried all his normal appendages.

The moon approached and was past; Earth was ahead. The blast of a warhead, a megaton at least, caught Barton off guard. The Demu shields blocked heat and other radiation, but the buffet dumped Barton out of his seat and slammed him against a wall, bad arm first. Cursing, he clawed his way back to the controls.

Evasive action was skittering zigzag toward Earth; Barton did it, while fiddling frantically with the communications controls. Not too much chance that Earth and Demu frequencies or modulation systems would match up, but worth trying.

From outside the ship he could hear nothing but incoherent noise. He figured it was probably the same at the other end, but he kept talking anyway.

"This is a captured alien ship. For Chrissakes don't

blow it up; it wasn't all that easy to get. God DAMmit!"—
as another warhead went off near him—"I said I captured
this thing. I stole it; you need it. Lay off the stupid fire-
works . . . " and so on. There was no sign that anyone
was paying attention.

With artificial gravity, he didn't have to mess around
with the gradual approach. Barton guessed that the shield-
effect would keep him from getting fried; he hit air in a
full dive. He scared himself by the narrow margin he had
left when he pulled out level. But at least he was down
where nobody could get a clear shot at him, and with
enough speed to beat anything local that he knew about.

He was over the Pacific; that was all he could tell about
the geography. It was either dawn or sunset; he'd lost
orientation after that second blast. Barton bet on dawn
because he didn't know how to fly the ship near the surface
in the dark. He hoped he was right, because he didn't
know how to speak Chinese, either.

Meanwhile he kept saying things like "All I want to do is
land this bastard and let somebody look it over. My name
is Barton and I used to *live* here." Somebody was ham-
mering on the other side of the control-room door, wanting
in. Somebody could go to hell, the way discipline seemed
to have done around here. Out in space where he could
leave the controls and move around, no one had bothered
him this way. Barton decided he'd make a lousy drill
sergeant; his teachings didn't seem to stick very well.

A voice came over the comm-gear; someone on the
ground (a computer, more likely) had decoded the Demu
modulation pattern and matched it. Probably hitting every
frequency band in reach, Barton suspected. "Calling the
human on the Raider ship," the voice said. "Are you in
control of that ship? Come in, please."

"Yeah, yeah," said Barton. "I got the ship; where do I
put it?" His relief was so great that the event hardly reg-
istered: that this was the first contact he'd had with Earth
since the Demu had taken him. How many years had it
been? He had no idea.

A nervous laugh came from the other end. "You sound
human enough, all right," the voice said. "Are you alone?"

"Hell no; I brought the Tenth Marines with me, band and
all. What did you think, dummy?" Barton caught himself.

"Sorry; I'm a little bent out of shape. No, I'm not alone, but I'm in charge. I have two of the Demu—the Raiders, you call them; I guess they've been back here some?—as prisoners. Take it easy on the little one; she's just a kid. Hasn't done anything, that I know of, to have taken out on her. The big one, her old man, was Director of the research station that carved up the other three on here, that used to look like us but don't any more. To him you can do any damn thing you want, except kill him: that's my privilege; don't anybody forget it." Barton caught himself just short of fully raving.

"OK," he said, "will somebody talk me in to land this bucket someplace, please?"

"Are you low on fuel or anything?"

"No." Low on patience, maybe, but he didn't say it.

The voice talked him in. The Demu instruments he knew how to operate, lacking Demu ground-based locator equipment, were no good to him. Local radar spotted his position and course so that he could be told how and when to turn, when to slow down, and what to look for at the designated landing site. He had guessed right on the dawn part; they brought him down somewhere in New Mexico. It was about noon there.

Barton sweat the landing, but the ship turned out to be practically foolproof; he was sure he was overcontrolling, but it touched ground gently. The Demu shield helped, he supposed. He felt the large muscles in his neck and shoulders relax almost explosively, and only then realized how tense he had been.

But maybe this was no time to relax. The outsider viewer showed him a lot of tanks and artillery surrounding him at close range, so he was in no hurry to chop the ship's protective field. "What the hell is all the hardware for?" he asked rather plaintively.

"Well, you must realize we can't take any chances, Barton."

Barton laughed right out loud; he couldn't help it. "Buddy, you're taking chances right now you don't even know about. You don't have any choice, come to that. I can help your odds. And get this: *I'm* not taking any chances at all. I don't have to; I've done that bit." He thought a minute, aimed a device and briefly activated it.

"That big hunk of gun off to my left," he said. It was the largest of the lot, that he could see. "Tell 'em to point that at me; just to point it. And see what happens."

Barton waited. Nothing happened, because he had used the Demu unconsciousness weapon on that gun crew. He had to make his point, and sometimes it takes a while. Patiently he waited until the voice channel quieted.

"All right," he said finally, "somebody has to trust somebody and I will if you will. Can we can the crap now and get to it?"

"What do you want?" The voice was tense and a little shaky.

"Nothing much. Just get the hardware off me and I'll keep mine off you. There have to be some big wheels out there someplace who want to talk. I want to talk with them, too, because I damn well have news for them. So if they'll come here to this ship I'll come out and meet 'em, and bring my zoo with me. We can talk, and it's perfectly safe for everybody unless some damn fool tries to cross me."

"I don't understand that last part, Barton."

"Be your age." He was dealing with paranoids, he told himself, so he had to fit the part. As though he didn't, already . . . "I push one button and we have a three-hundred-mile crater around here. I'll have the button in my hand." He heaved a sigh of exasperation. "Can we just talk now, instead?"

Barton had no such button. But he knew that sometimes a man has to bluff a little.

He shut off the voice channel: best to quit while he was ahead. Systematically he checked through the control assembly of switches, across and down, deactivating all but standby power to the ship. He was struck, wistfully, by the fact that he'd never learned the functions of most of those switches—had never activated them, had never dared. Well, other people could tackle that job now, if things worked out.

Barton looked around the control room of his ship. Hell, it was like leaving home. Not that there was anything he needed or wanted to take along. His snappy two-piece outfit, much smudged, was the lot. Barton turned abruptly and joined the others in the main compartment.

There they sat, all in Demu robes. No way of knowing which had hammered on the control-room door at a crucial moment. Barton didn't ask; it made no difference.

"We're on Earth," he said. "We go out now, to meet the people. If you have anything you want to keep with you, bring it. Siewen, Limila; interpret."

Little was said. Siewen shrilled a few lobster phrases to Whosits and the Director. Limila sat looking starkly ahead. Whnee scuttled to her bunk and picked up a few items to tuck into her robe. Barton wondered whether the others were out of brains or merely out of ears. So he repeated himself, only louder.

It took a while, but eventually Barton herded everyone out of the Demu ship to talk to the home folks. He faced a General Parkhurst, a Presidential Assistant Tarleton of the Space Agency and a bevy of news-media types among the trailing retinue. Barton put thumbs-down on the newsies. "Get those bastards out of here," he said. "They never get anything right in their lives, the first time. This is too important to let them fuck it up. Later, maybe, but not right now." But he was too late to stop them from taking pictures of the two Demu and the three pseudo-Demu. Not that it mattered all that much, probably, but it did bother him.

General Parkhurst was a small dapper man; his idea of efficiency was to do everything in a hurry. He took several reels of taped notes in the first hour. Then he departed abruptly while Barton was still trying to explain the difference between the Demu and his other companions. Barton shrugged and didn't miss him much.

The civilian, Tarleton, was a different bucket of clams, a big sloppy slow-talking bear of a man. He asked and he listened and he observed, without trying to tell Barton what to do. Barton had all his passengers shuck their robes and hoods to show themselves, whether they liked it or not.

The director was apparently quite indifferent to being paraded before an alien species. Of course his upper limbs were still strapped into splint-harnesses, so there wasn't much he could have done about it.

The smaller Demu shrank timidly until Barton patted it on the head and said "Whnee" in a gentle, encouraging tone of voice. Then it displayed its chitinous protrusionless exoskeleton in relative confidence. Barton had unsplinted its healed arm some time ago, and also Whosits'; he still didn't care to trust the Director that far.

"These are the Demu, the race we're up against," he said. "The big one ran the show at our zoo, as I said before, and it's the daddy or mother or something of the little one, if you can figure out how. She's his egg-child, anyway. What that means I don't know; they haven't said."

"It might imply more than one method of reproduction," Tarleton said mildly, talking around the stem of his unlighted pipe. "Now how about these others?"

"Two of them used to be human males," Barton began. "The skinny one with nothing between his legs is a Doktor Siewen; they amputated his spirit too, I think. Whosits there won't talk anything but Demu, so I don't know his name; supposedly he's still male, but not much of one by the looks of him."

Tarleton looked closely at the pertinent parts of Whosits, something Barton preferred not to do. There was a sort of nubbin; it might still work, at that. Hardly seemed worth it, though.

"There's no fertility," Tarleton said, "or won't be for long. Apparently one gonad is left, tucked neatly back into the abdominal cavity. The Demu must not have realized that this would produce sterility and eventual impotence." Whosits' serrated lips twitched but he said nothing.

"This is Limila," Barton said then. "She's a woman of a humanoid race much like ours: the Tilari."

"A woman?" Tarleton said slowly.

"Hell yes," Barton said. "Use your eyes; they didn't cut her butt off." He toned his voice down; he hadn't meant to shout. "Dammit, she was beautiful, Tarleton. Different from us, several ways. An extra toe and finger she had, all around. Forty teeth. Breasts set down low like so"— he gestured—"forehead clear up here by the ears. But beautiful. And mostly our kind of people.

"Why for Chris'sakes, Tarleton," he said, mind jarred back to the bloody death of the other Tilari woman, whose name he'd never known, "they're even interfertile with us." His jaw locked. "Don't ask me how I know. Not just yet."

Tarleton didn't ask. Unlike General Parkhurst, he seemed to sense that at the moment Barton was something like a time bomb coming to term, needing careful, patient defusing. Barton was dimly thankful for the man's presence.

Tarleton motioned the five exhibits to resume their robes, and directed the laying out of food and drink he'd ordered earlier. Apparently he did not see any of the five as human; he hadn't addressed a word to them.

"Can the Demu eat our food?" he asked.

"Damned if I know," Barton answered. "All I ever saw them eat, and all they ever fed me, was liquids and several kinds of wet lumpy glop. If they can't eat our stuff there's plenty of theirs on the ship. Siewen can fetch it."

The Demu ate Earth food all right, chewing with their hard sawtooth lips. But the other three couldn't manage anything except liquids and "glop" foods; their lips looked lobsterlike but chewing was out of the question. So Siewen was sent to the ship for Demu rations.

There was a hassle when the military guard, left by General Parkhurst, didn't want to admit Doktor Siewen. Tarleton intervened before the guard shot Barton, who was heading for the ship.

"Get that sonofabitch away from my ship!" Barton exploded. "Who the hell does Parkhurst think he is?"

"Easy now," Tarleton said mildly. "The General naturally tends to think in terms of security. The guard doesn't realize that you, of course, have free access." He motioned the guard away to one side, where he wouldn't bug Barton.

"Any more of this crap," Barton continued, "and Earth can go whistle. We'll see if maybe the Tilari, Limila's people, have a better idea of how to use a ship." He did not see Limila cringe.

"It'll be all right now, Barton," Tarleton said. "Come on; have something to eat. You'll feel better."

And in truth Barton did. He hadn't realized how much he'd missed the smells, tastes and textures of his own planet's foods, all the years he'd spent in a Demu cage.

For the first time, he thought to ask how long it had been. The answer was a little less than eight years. Barton repeated the current date. "What d'ya know?" he said. "I was forty a couple of weeks ago. Could have had a birthday party if I'd known." He grimaced. "Yeah, sure. Some party!" But Tarleton was talking on a radiophone link to someone he addressed as "sir," and only nodded absently.

After lunch a lanky technician insisted on taking fingerprints. He didn't seem too put out that Demu fingers had no recognizable patterns, but was a little upset that no one except Barton had enough fingers to fill all the blanks on his forms. Barton tried to explain that Limila's prints couldn't possibly be on file; the man grinned, and drawled, "Orders, buddy." He was so phlegmatic about it that Barton merely shrugged. Tarleton relaxed visibly.

Whosits' prints were taken by main force while he protested shrilly in lobster language, but the Demu made no such complaints. The Director certainly didn't; Barton had finally unstrapped his arms in honor of his first Earthly meal, and the Director was experiencing freedom of movement for the first time in a long while. Twinges and all, probably. Barton kept an eye on him at first; then he got tired of the necessity and went into the ship. He came out with a small device necessary to the operation of the controls; even if the Director managed to sneak onto the ship, he couldn't get away with it. If the Director had had the sense to do the same thing at the far end of the ride, Barton thought, things could have been rough.

Tarleton was trying to explain what the problem was. Bureaucrats and administrators with the habit of explaining to Barton what the problem was had helped him decide to drop physics and take up painting. But this man seemed like a sensible sort, so Barton decided he'd better listen.

"The problem is," Tarleton said, "that we need to study the ship, and quite near here is the best facility for that purpose. Also we need to study the Demu and—er—the others, and a hospital on the East Coast is best for that. In Maryland, as it happens. But," he concluded, "the hell of it is that we need the Demu, the big one at least, on hand here for information about the ship."

"Yeh, and Siewen and Limila to interpret," Barton added.

"Precisely. Any ideas?"

"Well, just offhand, Tarleton, I'd say a medical or life-study lab is a lot easier to move than the stuff it's going to take to check out this ship. And if anything goes wrong, like maybe blowing up the whole schmeer, you want a lot of empty country around. You're not going to find that in Maryland."

Tarleton looked at him obliquely. "Speaking of things blowing up, how about that button in your pocket? The three-hundred-mile-crater button you mentioned earlier?"

Barton grinned sheepishly. "No such animal," he admitted. "All it was, those fogheads had a lot of guns aimed at me and I didn't like it." He was surprised to see the shudder that shook Tarleton; he hadn't realized the man had been so tense under his slow easygoing exterior. "I'm sorry," Barton said. "I'd have said something before, but I forgot all about it."

"That's OK," the big man said. "Let's get to work figuring things out." He ran Barton through the high points of his story again; he got on the phone to D.C. several times. He even questioned Siewen briefly, though it was obvious he would have felt as much at ease interviewing a giant grasshopper.

Then it was time for another meal. Afterward Barton was really and truly pooped out of his mind. It was hard to tell a coherent story, leaving out the hallucinations, and Barton figured he'd better not tell anybody about that part. Not ever.

Some improvised quarters in kit form had arrived by truck and were in process of assembly, but Barton said the hell with that. "We'll sleep on the ship. I'm used to it, and the guards can make sure nobody goes sleepwalking."

Tarleton didn't like the idea too well, so Barton showed him the locking device he'd removed from the ship. "Here, these are the keys to the car. You hold 'em for tonight." He looked the other man in the eyes. "I guess you know what this means: I have to trust you a lot. I wouldn't want anyone else, like that Parkhurst, to get his hands on this gadget. OK?" Tarleton nodded, and Barton shepherded his charges aboard for the night. After eight years or so, that was Barton's first day back on Earth.

The next few days were hectic but inconclusive. Quarters were erected for the research people who were being moved in, as well as for Barton and his entourage. There was a hassle the second day when Limila refused to be quartered anywhere at all away from Barton; they settled in a two-bedroom unit not far from Siewen and Whosits and the two Demu. The latter had a larger unit, built much the same. Except that there was no guard on Barton's quarters.

Portable lab buildings were brought to the site, and truckloads of gear with which to equip them. The ship itself, Barton at the controls, was moved to the vicinity of a complex of buildings about five kilometers away, behind a low range of hills. Fat lot of good that would do, Barton thought, but kept his reservations to himself.

And eventually General Parkhurst trundled his guns and tanks back to the nearby Army base he commanded.

Trickles of response began to come in from the outside world. Barton's fingerprints were verified, and Doktor Siewen's; Whosits' were not on file in any country lending cooperation. Barton hoped no one had wasted much effort looking for Limila's.

Barton got a post-mortem on his own former personal life. His father had died five years ago, and his mother a few months later; he had no siblings or other close relatives. Seven years after his disappearance Barton had been declared legally dead. His ex-wife and her new husband were living well, helped somewhat by his estate, since his paintings had gradually become popular enough to be valuable. His ex-mistress, Leonie, had married and gained four children, plus ten or fifteen pounds of weight for each of them.

Well, it was all pretty much as he'd expected. Par for the course. Barton could find no emotional reaction in himself; it was as though his former life were someone else's—a total stranger's.

Tarleton assured him that while his estate was legally out of reach, a grateful government would see to his financial well-being. Barton would believe that when he saw it, but the keys to the car were in his own pockets again and he hadn't signed anything yet, he reminded himself. He requested a small safe for his bedroom and set his own combination; the keys were secure enough for now.

Idly, once, he guessed at the value of the Demu ship in terms of ransom for the planet Earth. Then he shrugged, and moved a mental decimal point four places to the left. He'd be lucky to get a dime over living expense and a consultant fee, but no harm in trying. Besides, he wanted to see the chintzy bastards sweat when he hit 'em with the big numbers. Just for kicks; he hadn't had many of those in the past eight years.

Doktor Siewen's middle-aged son and daughter sent their kindest personal regards. They were *so* glad their father was alive and safe, but Barton noticed they didn't offer to visit him or vice versa. He suspected they'd seen those first news pics, before the government had suppressed the story. Siewen didn't seem to notice, or care.

And still there was no word on Whosits. Maybe Siewen had been wrong; maybe Whosits wasn't of Earth origin after all. Well, who cared? Not Barton, for sure!

Tarleton filled him in on what Earth knew of the Demu, the "Raiders."

"The ship that got you was spotted on radar, but nobody believed it. It was too big." Barton gave him an estimate of the size of the larger ships he'd seen at the Demu research station. Tarleton said the radar had shown something a lot bigger. Barton wondered if the protective shield could have bollixed the readings. Tarleton shrugged. "We can check that out when it's time for you to fly this one for us next." That was OK with Barton.

"We have no idea how many people that ship took," Tarleton continued, "because every day, all over the world, people disappear. Some are murdered, some are accidents and suicides, some disappear deliberately. But the best estimate is that the Demu got at least several hundred."

Barton looked surprised. Tarleton raised his eyebrows. "Well, of course," he said, "you saw only the people— including those not of this planet—in your own, er, cage. A ship of the size you indicate could have contained many such.

"The Raiders, the Demu, have been back twice since then." That too was news to Barton, though he'd guessed something of the sort when he first heard the term "Raiders." "Once about four years ago; they must have taken over a thousand that time. And then roughly two years later." Tarleton smiled grimly. "That time we were ready, or thought we were. With the high-G rockets and warheads, like the ones thrown at you when you came in. The Pentagon still claims they got that ship, but judging from the results with yours I'd guess the Demu were merely startled and cautious, and withdrew for the time being.

"Well, with luck and a good analysis of your ship, Barton, we may be in a considerably better position to handle them, next time they turn up."

Barton nodded. That was what he had in mind. For starters.

Research got under way so unobtrusively that Barton hardly noticed how quickly it developed. On the ship and its weapons, on the Demu, on Siewen and Limila and Whosits. And then, as he had known it must, on Barton.

The physical exams were all right. He was organically sound, he was told, and had been living with a lower background-radiation level than Earth's. He took the offer to have his lumpy arm rebroken and set to heal straight; he had it done with a shoulder block rather than a general anesthetic. The cast was light and didn't bother him half as much as the unset break had for so long.

His teeth needed some work. All right; dental care was available at Parkhurst's Army base. Novocaine though, not gas.

He was questioned repeatedly and in detail, by persons and teams of several specialties. Considering that he had to edit a number of important details out of his experiences, he told a fairly straight story. What he omitted was of a personal nature, mostly: the two mutilated women who had successively shared his cage, and some of his stronger reactions both before and after escaping. And of course, any mention of self-hypnosis or hallucination. The only mental irregularities he admitted were the temporary memory-loss effects of the Demu sleep gun.

He had devised, he thought, a fairly credible explanation of his escape: that in the absence of any better idea he'd formed the habit of lying on the food-service area of the floor after meals, and that once, finally, the thing had malfunctioned and let him through.

Everyone bought it, except the psychology boys. Dr. Roderick Skinner, acting head of the branch in the absence of a Dr. Fox, called on Barton one afternoon. Limila was elsewhere, being interviewed. Skinner carried a briefcase, from which he extracted an untidy clipboard. "Barton, I'll tell you frankly that I'm not yet satisfied with the total picture." Barton waved him to a chair.

"Yeh, well, sit down. Be with you in a minute." He went to the kitchen, opened a can of beer. He thought for a moment and decided what the hell, he might as well waste a beer on this clown in the interests of public relations. He didn't ask, but merely brought another one out and handed it to the psychologist. "OK, shoot. What don't you like?"

"That's the trouble, Barton; I'm not certain. Everything *seems* to check, but the data do not quite explain the reported events."

"Well, I've told you everything I can." That much was true, Barton thought; he carefully had not said he'd told everything he remembered. He savored the difference.

"We ran it through the computer, Barton, and we keep getting nulls in the output. Any idea why?"

"Not my line. What's your idea?"

"That there are nulls in the input—in your report. So we're going to have to check for them."

"If you have any new questions, ask away. I've answered the old ones enough times, I think."

"It's not a matter of new questions. It's a matter of confirming your answers to the ones we've already asked."

"You want to look at the Demu research station yourself? Bon voyage, Skinner; it's a long trip."

Skinner's laugh wasn't convincing. "No, we'll do our checking right here, Barton. With you."

"OK; get on with it, then."

"I didn't mean *right* here, actually. The necessary drugs are best administered in the laboratory under controlled conditions."

"Drugs?" Controlled conditions—Barton had had enough of those! He went rigid inside. "What the hell are you talking about?"

"A simple hypnotic, Barton. Quite harmless. We think that some crucial memories are hiding out in your subconscious mind, and we must get them out in the open, for analysis."

"Not with hypnotics, you don't. Not on *me*. The Demu—"

"I'm afraid we have to; you see—"

"You have to *shit*, too, if you eat regular! No dice, Skinner. You take your drugs and—"

"I think you forget who you're talking to!"

"And I think you forgot where you are. You're in *my* place. Get out."

"It won't do you any good to be hostile, Barton. I can have you *brought* in to the labs, you know."

That did it. "Like *this?*" He grabbed Skinner, pulled him upright, spun him around. The man was yammering; Barton didn't listen. He aimed Skinner at the door. He didn't exactly throw him out or kick him out, either one; it was a combination of both. The door was open but the screen wasn't. Nothing fatal, but messy. "And *stay* out, you son of a bitch!"

Skinner wouldn't be back, but Barton knew he was in the soup, for sure.

He had stalled off all requests to take mental tests, but now he'd blown it. He went looking for Tarleton, trying to think of an excuse to get the man to take the heat off him, but he was in D.C. briefing the President or something. Barton thought again. Dr. Fox, whose minion he had thrown through the screen, was arriving the next day. Barton decided to be one of her first customers, and, next morning, was.

Dr. Arleta Fox was a compact woman in her thirties, with frizzy auburn hair and a face like that of an especially attractive Pekingese. Her smile was friendly but made Barton wonder if he were really out of range of a fast snap. She asked him what the problem was. Well, that was a nice switch.

"Your boy wanted to poke hypnotics into me," Barton said. "I got mad and threw him out."

"Yes, I believe he mentioned that," Dr. Fox said, with considerable understatement. "What's your twistup on hypnotics, Mr. Barton? You know we have to get all the subliminal data you may have—things you saw without noticing that you saw them."

"I had enough different kinds of dope from the lobsters to last me," said Barton. "In my food, in the air:

you name it; I had it. I don't need any more. I tried to tell Skinner, but he wouldn't listen."

"He had his orders, Mr. Barton." The smile. Unconsciously, Barton pulled his hand back. "Perhaps that was my mistake. But you see, we have no real psychological data on you at all, more recent than eight years ago before all this happened, so I had no way of knowing there would be a problem." Barton nodded, but said nothing.

"I'll make a bargain with you, Mr. Barton. As I said, we have no recent psychological information on you, whatsoever. If you'll take the standard battery of tests, over the next few days, we'll shelve the question of using hypnotics."

"For how long?" Barton asked.

"Indefinitely. Until you give your consent. Whatever you say."

"Never, then. It's a deal, Doctor. Thanks." Barton stood up.

"Here tomorrow morning at nine sharp, Mr. Barton? We'll provide pencil and paper."

Barton smiled, nodded and went out, surprised to note how heavily he was sweating. Well, he wasn't out of the woods by any means, but maybe he had a chance. At least they couldn't open his mind and see what was there, that not even Barton knew about for sure. He wasn't ready to look at that stuff himself, and he knew it. Meanwhile he didn't want anyone else grabbing a sneak preview.

He caught a ride to the ship. Nothing much doing there: they were still piddling around snipping off bits of materials for analysis. At this rate, Barton thought, the ship was going to look as though it had been gnawed by mice, before the government in its infinite wisdom actually got around to seeing what the damn thing would do.

However, he had one pleasant surprise. Kreugel, Tarleton's crew chief for ship operations, greeted him. "Hey, Mr. Barton! I think we're going to get the handle on the artificial gravity, and that's not more than a jump or two from their space drive."

Barton was flabbergasted. "Now how in hell did you manage *that?*"

"When we learned how to read the circuit diagrams and equipment drawings, it turned out to be awfully close to what the Space Agency labs have been working on for the past three-four years. Close enough that I think we've nearly got it whipped."

"Hey, hold it," said Barton. "*What* circuit diagrams? And how did you learn to read them, anyway?" He felt as though he were in a play and hadn't read the script.

"They're built into the viewscreen circuits." Barton felt like a damn fool; why hadn't *he* dug up any of this stuff, in the months he'd had?

"You wouldn't have found them," Kruegel went on, "because the switches that throw the schematics on the screen won't work when you're under power, without throwing a special cutover switch that doesn't give any indication until you do move the circuit-diagram controls. You wouldn't have hit the combination by random chance in a long time even if you'd been playing games on the board, and in your shoes I don't imagine you felt much like doing that." Barton's ego pulled its socks up a little.

"So how did you find it?"

"Well, Mr. Barton, you know we've been interrogating Hishtoo, the bigger crawdaddy, with that poor devil Siewen interpreting. Some of our other people are trying to learn the Demu language so we can work faster, but so far they're getting nowhere fast." So the Director's name was Hishtoo; how about that? Or something that sounded like Hishtoo. "Well, when we asked where the devil the tech manuals were for this beast here, he got cagey and wouldn't talk. So Mr. Tarleton put a hammerlock on him and leaned on it and said something about crab salad, and Hishtoo began talking and just plain wouldn't stop." Barton grinned, not a nice grin. So Tarleton had paid attention to his report—the early version—after all. Crab salad, yet!

"Well, good on Tarleton," was all he said. "Stick with it; you're doing great." He wandered around a little and decided to go back to his quarters. There was no vehicle handy, so he walked it. Sweating in the hot sun felt good, for a change.

Back at the quarters he hesitated, hating to enter. Limila seldom spoke to him lately except in answer to a direct question; her silent withdrawal was hard to take. He supposed she responded to the interrogations of the data-gathering team, or someone would have told him what the problem was. He shrugged and went inside.

He didn't see or hear Limila at first. The tri-V was blaring; he turned the sound low. Then he heard her, in her own bedroom. He opened the door a few inches and saw her as well. Curled into a tight ball in the middle of her bed, she was crying in great racking sobs. After a moment he shook his head, closed the door gently and turned away. There was nothing he could do.

He poured himself the stiffest damn drink he could manage, and watched the stupidities of tri-V. The 3-D picture was new to him, but the content of the medium hadn't improved a bit in eight years, or since he could remember, in fact. If anything, it was getting worse. Or maybe it was he who was getting worse . . .

Barton opened a package of tri-V-advertised prepared food, heated it and ate it. The taste, when he noticed it, was about like that of a well-composted pile of mulch.

Returning to his drink and ignoring the tri-V, Barton ran in his own head the ultimate tri-V commercial he could imagine.

"Eat Mushie-Tushies," it went, "the truly effort-free food! Mushie-Tushies are pre-cooked, pre-chewed, pre-swallowed, pre-digested and pre-excreted! Just heat them up and throw them down the toilet!" Barton finished his drink, turned off the tri-V, and went to his own bed. He caught himself short of slamming the bedroom door; Limila might be asleep. Whether she was or not, the thought of her kept Barton awake another hour, not pleasantly.

Next morning he was at Dr. Fox's office at nine sharp, as agreed. Not one second late; that was his commitment to her. Not more than five seconds early; that was his commitment to himself. Nine sharp, as nearly as he could manage.

Dr. Fox smiled continually. Barton didn't listen closely to what she said or to what he answered; it was small talk and not relevant. Bla-bla-bla, she said in polite tones. Bla-bla-indeed, he answered gravely, equally polite. Maybe it even made some sort of sense.

When she got down to cases, he paid attention. First there would be a simple IQ test. Well, not a simple test, but a test simply for the measurement of his intelligence. OK; he presumed he had some of that left and he didn't mind if they measured it.

The test was part verbal and part written, and all of it no sweat. Barton's memories, which had been suppressed and foggy early in his captivity, and spotty for nearly all of it, had begun coming back more rapidly since his escape. He and Tarleton had discussed the phenomenon early in their acquaintance, in light of the fact that memory suppression was a side-effect of the Demu unconsciousness weapon. The gun crew Barton had zapped when he first arrived had been pretty foggy-minded for several days afterward. And the Demu had used the gadget on Barton a number of times, while they had him.

But now his logic and memory circuits were, so far as he could tell, in reasonably good order. He breezed through the many sections of the test, not giving much of a damn how he came out on it but still giving honest answers when he could settle on any answer at all. And in most cases, he could.

The test was a long one; it was past noon when he finished and time for lunch. He and Dr. Fox said smiling bla-blas at each other while they ate, until she mentioned that next on the agenda was a battery of personality-evaluation tests.

Barton knew what that meant. They would rate him on or off the permissible scales of Aggressive-Submissive, Masculine-Feminine, Dependent-Independent—oh yes, the whole set of categories that he could not possibly fit correctly from where he stood, after nearly eight years in a cage. What it added up to was a rating of Sane-Insane. Barton knew he would flunk.

"And which tests are you using, Doctor?" he asked. She named the series. It was unfamiliar to him, but a book of that title caught his eye, on a shelf not too far out of his reach. I think, thought Barton, it is time I had a bad attack of the clumsies.

"Could I have another cup of coffee?" he asked. Pre-creamed pre-sugared instant crud, but he didn't say so. Dr. Fox poured it for him and handed him the cup. He dropped it, spilling the liquid toward a stack of papers on her desk.

©Lorillard 1973

Micronite filter.
Mild, smooth taste.
America's quality
cigarette.
Kent.

KENT
WITH
THE FAMOUS MICRONITE FILTER

DELUXE LENGTH

King Size or Deluxe 100's.

Try the crisp, clean taste of Kent Menthol.

The only Menthol with the famous Micronite filter.

His apparent effort to save the papers pushed them off the edge. He and she both dived to save them; their heads hit squarely. Barton was braced for it, so while the lady got her eyes back in focus and her jaw back up where it belonged, he neatly lifted the book he wanted and tucked it down the front of his trousers. Then he helped her up, helped her pick up the papers and mop up the mess.

"Hey, I *am* sorry, Doctor," he said. "I guess my co-ordination still isn't what it should be." He paused. "You all right? Me, I think I'm getting a headache. You suppose we could put this next one off until tomorrow?"

Dr. Fox hadn't had a chance. Nine sharp? No, you'd better make that one p.m. Bla-bla, smile, see you to-morrow. Barton hoped without malice that she was too woozy to wonder how a man could pilot and land an alien spaceship, who on solid ground couldn't keep from spilling his coffee.

He went directly home. Limila wasn't around; she was probably with the interrogation team. At the moment he felt he could use the absence of personality pressure.

Barton had to beat those goddam tests or they'd have him, for sure; he knew it. Several times since his return to Earth he'd caught himself just short of assaulting some-one he found excessively annoying. With intent to commit mayhem. He knew this was not unusual in the overcrowded cultures of Earth; he also knew it was grounds for getting locked up.

Barton had been in a cage for a long time; he was not about to be locked into another one. *That* was what the problem was.

For starters, he took the tests honestly (he'd gambled that sample copies and grading instructions were in the book; they were). The answers he got were about what he had expected; Barton was not safe to have at large, even to himself. Well, he'd have to chance that, the same as he'd been doing for some time. As for other people—well, he figured he'd taken his own chances long enough that it wasn't out of line for others to share them now. He knew no one else would see it that way, though it should be obvious that anyone who did away with the tri-V announcer, for instance, deserved a bonus . . . Oh well.

Looking at the summaries of "preferred" (sane) an-

swers, Barton knew he couldn't possibly memorize enough
of the responses to give a reasonable picture of a man
with his head on straight; it couldn't be done. But there
had to be a way.

The series of tests ran to a total of over 1,300 mul-
tiple-choice questions: five choices per question. The odds
against him were incalculable. But what about a random
approach? Barton looked around the room.

A pair of ornamental dice sat on a low table. Barton
took one die in his hand. Six choices: #1 through #5, the
answers to any question on the test. #6, leave it blank.

Barton threw the die and marked the result for each
of the 107 questions on the first test. Then he turned again
to the Evaluations section. Hopeless.

"These results indicate either a fragmented incoherent
mind or a highly irresponsible attitude. In either case there
is urgent need of custody and therapy." OK, OK, he
thought; I've already bagged that idea.

Barton's situation didn't need a drink, but he did. He
mixed it about half as heavy as he really wanted it. He
sat down in front of the tri-V set, thought about turning
it on, then got up and carefully turned the bulky heavy
thing around to face directly into the wall. At that point,
Limila came in.

As usual she did not speak. Barton had long since quit
offering unanswered greetings, though he knew he needed
to talk with her and maybe vice versa. In fact she was the
only person he knew that he *could* talk to, about a lot
of things. But that problem would have to wait.

She got herself some food and took it into her bedroom, softly closing the door behind her. Barton ached,
thinking of how she must feel at what had been done to
her. But he shrugged it off; he had to, just then. He ranged
around the place, looking for something to spark his mind
toward a way to beat those damned tests and stay out of
a cage. Because he wouldn't go. Not again, he wouldn't.

His eye was caught by the supply of canvases and paints
in the far dimmest corner of the room. He'd asked for the
materials several days ago but hadn't used them yet.
Maybe it was time he did; it struck him that sometimes
the hands can tell the mind what it really means.

Barton arranged the easel, the canvas, the palette and

brushes, the lights. He hadn't painted for eight years; he had no idea what he was going to do. But he needed to do it; he knew that much. Barton blurred his mind and began. Working, he lost track of time.

A sound behind him brought him out of it. A harsh accusing sound. Barton turned and saw Limila, sawtooth lips squared in an almost-human grimace of horror, blank Demu lack of features throwing the horror back to him. She shook her head, the bald earless skull shining in the overhead light. "No more, Barton," she panted. "No MORE!" She wheeled and disappeared through her bedroom door, slamming it and throwing the bolt against him. As though there were any need for that, he thought sadly.

But what had caused her reaction? Barton looked at his canvas and gasped in shock. What he had painted, what he had doodled while his mind looked the other way, was Limila. Limila the undefiled, as he had first seen her. Several views. Two full-faced, one with closed curved-lip smile and one showing the tiny perfect teeth. A profile highlighting the delicate lean nose and over-the-ears front hairline. A pair of complementing three-quarter studies. Two full-length figures. And each sketch, though lacking in fine detail, was lovingly exact in contour. No wonder Limila could not bear to see them.

Barton turned his ears on. It was about time he did that; the noises from Limila's room were not nice. He took a run at her door, jumped and landed with both heels alongside the door knob. The lock broke; Barton sprawled inside, to see Limila turning and twisting as she hung with her neck in an impromptu noose.

He never knew how he clawed her down from her ad-lib gibbet, though several shredded fingernails took long enough to heal. He gave mouth-to-mouth breathing to the sawtooth lips he had not been able to bring himself to kiss since the Demu had cut their sweet curves into harsh notches. He said her name over and over. And when he saw that she was conscious and could hear him, he said to her, "Don't ever do that again. I need you; do you understand me?" She nodded, weakly.

"Limila," he said, "I don't know yet what we can do about how things are. But I'll work on it. You hear me?"

"You can do nothing. I am as I am." Her eyes were closed. Barton shook her, gently, until she opened them.

"And the Demu had me in a cage for eight years," he said. "I thought my way out of that one, or we wouldn't be here, would we?" She looked at him blankly. "Give me a little time, won't you? To try to find a way out of the cage *we* are in."

The mangled lips twisted in what might have been a smile. Barton blotted it from sight by kissing her smooth forehead. He held her for a moment longer and then said, "Forgive me. For hiding from you, for not paying attention because it hurt to see you. I won't do that any more. You understand?" Her head nodded against his lips. He got up slowly, turned away, stopped at the shattered door. "I'll do *something*."

Barton slept without pills; his dreams were not of horror. And he woke knowing what he had to do next, to stay out of a cage.

At one o'clock he met Dr. Arleta Fox. All of ten seconds early, in fact; under the circumstances Barton felt he could afford to give a little. He put the pilfered book back in place under cover of clumsily dropping his jacket when he hung it up; Barton knew he had to clown it a little and he figured he could get away with that much. Dr. Fox was tolerant.

"Don't be nervous, Mr. Barton," she said. "You needn't be. Your intelligence tests show no significant changes from the earlier data in your file. A slight drop of no importance. These tests are so sensitive that what you had for lunch could shift the results by five points, and that's approximately the degree of change we have here." Dr. Fox smiled. By now, Barton's subconscious knew she wasn't really going to bite him; he didn't flinch. "So now," she said brightly, "are we ready for the personality-evaluation series?"

I don't know about you, lady, thought Barton, but *I* sure's hell am. Because now he knew how to beat their system, for a while, at least. All he needed was a little cooperation.

"Sure, I'm ready," he said. "One thing, though. I'm a little nervous today. Could I have a closed room and no interruptions until I'm finished?" He tried to smile disarmingly. It didn't feel much like it, from the inside.

Dr. Fox bought it, at least. "Oh, certainly," she said, and escorted him to a small, comfortable room. With ashtrays and everything.

Ever since Barton had willed himself dead enough to fall through the floor of the Demu cage—all the way home on the ship and ever since—he had, with one exception, stayed clear of self-hypnosis and the hallucinations that had saved him from Demu domination and mutilation. Because he wasn't a captive mind any longer, and a free one can't afford to goof off if it wants to stay free. So Barton had tried to stick with the real world all the way.

But policy must change with circumstances. When Barton sat down to fill out the 1,300-plus questions of the personality-evaluation tests, he shoved his mind into full-hallucinating gear. What he tried to bring into being was the thirty-two-year-old Barton and all his attitudes, before he had been zapped and abducted by the Demu. He knew it was a pretty thin trick but it was the best he had. And it began to work. So be it.

Barton had no idea how long it was taking him to answer all the questions on Dr. Fox's fancy test; he stayed with it until he was finished. Then he snapped out of his earlier-Barton hallucination and paid very close attention to reality. He punched the buzzer; when Dr. Fox answered he told her he had finished and was ready to leave. The time turned out to be late evening; he'd skipped dinner and hadn't even noticed.

"Why don't we have a drink and a bite to eat in the lounge before you go, Mr. Barton?" she asked. Why don't we break open my skull and get it over with, Dr. Fox? But the hell with it; he had to go along, a little.

The lounge wasn't bad; the lighting and music were within his tolerance and Dr. Fox wasn't pushing him about anything. Barton ordered the strongest drink he figured he could get away with under psychological observation. He got a bonus; food service was so slow he had time for a second one. Partway into it he realized he couldn't afford to get smashed, either. But physically and mentally he was floating free, ready to move.

He wasn't surprised when one of the lumpier and more muscular of the young lab techs brought a sheaf of papers to Dr. Fox, whispering in her ear somewhat more than was really courteous. She began to leaf through the stack, skimming.

Barton figured they had him cold, but he wasn't going to make it easy. There was a pot of coffee on the table over a heater; he poured some for Dr. Fox.

For one thing, if he needed to throw the rest of it at Muscles' face it would be quicker if he already had the thing in his hand. So he held onto it for a moment, waiting to see what Dr. Fox would say.

She said it. "Mr. Barton, I can hardly believe these results." Barton wasn't too surprised but there wasn't much he could say. The technician left them. Barton returned the coffee pot to its place.

"Your test results," Dr. Fox continued, "are almost precisely the same as the way you tested eight years ago." She smiled, frowned, scowled and looked blank. It was like a major earthquake on a small scale, thought Barton.

"Our computer read-out," Dr. Fox went on, "allows only one conclusion. It indicates that your capture and imprisonment have inflicted a so-called 'freeze trauma' upon you. You appear to be frozen into your earlier emotional attitudes, without much reference to any happenings since the trauma began."

Well, if you'll believe that, Barton thought, you'll believe anything. But what he said was, "It doesn't feel that way to me, but I guess I can't argue with you experts, and the computer and all." Oddly, he found that he enjoyed skating on thin ice.

"The tests were really very tiring, Dr. Fox," he said. "The food is good but my appetite isn't up to it. I hate to be a poor guest, but if I don't go home and get some sleep about now, I'll probably cork off right here and have to be carted home." Dr. Fox was understanding and obliging; soon Barton was delivered to his quarters. Limila was still awake. Just sitting, looking at the walls.

"I was soon going to bed," she said. "I will now."

"All right," said Barton, "but not in there. In here."

At first Limila expected more than Barton was able to give. He could not make love to her mutilated self, nor did he try. But he could hold her and cherish her; they could give each other warmth. After a while, Limila appeared to understand how it was with them, how it had to be. She cried, but it did not hurt Barton as much as he expected. After a little longer it didn't hurt at all, because it was a different kind of crying. Whatever it was, he succumbed to sleep before he figured it out.

He woke up alone. Well, Limila would be over at the ship, helping with the translating. Tarleton and Kreugel had become wary of having only one translator. Frail and shaky as Siewen was becoming, no one knew how far he could be trusted.

Barton fixed himself breakfast. More real food was coming in lately, to replace the TV-dinner junk that had first been shipped to the site. He broke three eggs into the frying pan, thought a moment and added another. The bread was standard glop-type but not too bad when toasted. There was real coffee.

Idly, Barton wondered what to do next. Dr. Fox was off his back for a time; probably she knew something was fishy, but it would take her a while to get her nerve up to doubt the computer results. He wasn't needed at the ship immediately; someone would have told him. He'd like to get the cast off his arm, lightweight or not, but the doctors had told him not to pester them again for at least another week. It wasn't limiting his activities; it itched, was all.

When in doubt, he decided, take a walk. He'd never been much for gratuitous exercise Before, but now he found he liked to walk when he had the time for it. So he clothed himself and stepped outside. The day was hot and sunny, which was nothing new around here, but he liked it anyway.

His way took him past the quarters of the Demu and the Demu-ized. As he approached them, he wondered how and what little Whnee had been doing lately. At first he had looked in on her occasionally; she'd been pleased to see him, as near as he could tell. Then a couple of times she hadn't been at home; she was being studied by a research team. A little perturbed, he'd checked with Tarleton and been assured that the small Demu would not be

harmed. Then Barton had got busy with his own concerns
and had had no time for much of anything else.

As he passed the guarded house he saw Whnee looking
out a window. He was across the street, but he paused and
walked over. The guard said, "Yes, sir?"

"I'm Barton. I see the little Demu is at home today."

"Yes, sir. It and the Freak; he's here all the time,
though. The teams gave up on him." That would be Whosits. Well, Barton had given up on Whosits a long time ago.

"How about the young one? They give up on her too?"

"Oh no, sir," the guard answered, "they're pretty happy
about that one, the way I hear it. It's just their day off
today. Sunday, you know." Barton hadn't known. His
work and Tarleton's paid no heed to the weekly calendar,
so neither had he.

"I think I'll stop in and see the kid a minute," Barton
said. A thought came to him. "Hey, OK if we go out for
a little walk?"

"Just a moment, sir. I'll ask it." The guard turned and
entered the house, leaving Barton a little puzzled. *Ask* it?

A few minutes later, the guard escorted Whnee outdoors. No robe and hood now: Whnee was wearing a
small sunhat, a light loose garment that covered the torso
but left the limbs bare, and sandals. The lobster face
looked incongruous, but on the whole Barton liked the
effect. The standard Demu garb held bad connotations
for him, naturally enough.

"Hello, Whnee," he said.

"Hello, Barton. But my name is not Whnee. It is Eeshta."

"You talk English!"

Whnee's—Eeshta's—tongue lifted in the Demu smile.
"Yes, Barton. They have taught me. I wanted to learn. I
wanted to talk with you. Now we can talk."

Barton looked at the small lobsterlike Demu in its absurd
but pleasant Earth-type garb. Remembering. How its egg-
parent had kept Barton as a caged animal for years.
How he had broken this one's arm, slapped it into silence
and later, unconsciousness. How he had kidnapped both and
brought them to Earth as prisoners. He had treated this
small one with kindness or at least with tolerance during
the voyage, yes. But still he wondered what he and Whnee,

or Eeshta, had in common to discuss. It might be_ interesting to find out.

"OK," he said. "Want to come for a little walk?" He looked at the guard, who nodded and then looked after the oddly assorted pair as they moved away.

"I like your outfit," Barton said. "Kind of a change from the old one."

"Yes. That is out of place here, so I changed to this. Dr. Ling chose it." Dr. Ling? Oh, yes; Barton remembered. Female doctor, Chinese ancestry, in charge of the team studying Demu biology.

"Well, it looks fine, Whnee—I mean, Eeshta."

The smile again. "Call me Whnee if you like. Or Eeshta. Either is all right."

"Eeshta. I'll try to remember. Anyway, what-all else have you been learning?"

"Very much. Most important, that you are Demu."

"What?"

"That you are people. Demu is our only *word* for people. We are taught to believe that all others are animals."

"Yeh, I found that out the hard way. Not as hard as some others we know, of course."

"Barton, I am ashamed. For us, who call ourselves Demu. For what we do to others, treating them as animals. Because they do not speak our words. And when they do, we make them like Siewen and Limila and the Freak. I am glad you did not let us do that to you, Barton."

"You call him the Freak?"

"He is. He is one of you but pretends to be one of us. He wears the old clothing. He will not speak his own language. It is our fault, of course. We have broken him."

"Hell; you didn't do it."

"But if I had been older, I would have. I believed it was right, also."

"Well, we all do what we have to," Barton said. "I wasn't exactly gentle with you there at first, either. I can't see that I had much choice, but still I'm sorry you had to be hurt."

"So am I," Eeshta said. Barton looked at her sharply, but apparently it was a purely matter-of-fact comment. "Barton, I was so frightened then! Attacked by a vicious

animal, I thought. Injured and tied and beaten. Almost
I died of fright."

Barton started to say something but thought better of it.

"I first had hope, Barton, when you let me drink. You
could have not done that." Eeshta made a grimace Barton hadn't seen before on a Demu. "I am glad I did not
know your language then. If I had known you were saying
you would eat me alive, I am sure I would have died of
hearing it."

"Who—who told you about that?" Barton didn't bother
to deny it or say it had been a bluff. It had been, but
this was no time to expect her to believe it.

"Siewen," she said, "or Limila. I don't remember now.
It is not important." She looked at him. "What is important is that *we* made you do that. I am ashamed." Barton
had no answer. Hell, the kid was right, wasn't she? *It?* Nobody had told him the findings, if any, on the Demu, and
he'd been too busy to think to ask. Well, it might make
a good change of subject; the present one bothered him.

"Eeshta," he said, "what does it mean that you're
Hishtoo's egg-child? I mean, is there some other kind of
child, with you people?" She paused for a moment, stopped
walking. Barton thought it might be time to turn back;
they'd come quite a way.

"It seems strange to us, Barton, that you people are
male or female. Only one or the other, I mean. We are
both, all of us. But not so strongly, to see. That is why
we didn't understand, and spoiled Siewen and the Freak."
And Limila?

"I will show you," she said, and pulled up her garment,
baring the torso. Barton didn't see anything especially note-
worthy, only the flexible chitinous body shell, with the
little bumps and dimples up the front.

"Look closer, Barton," Eeshta said. "See the small
raised portions, and the indented places? How they make
a pattern up the middle of me there, thus-wide?"

He nodded, thinking: "So *that's* what the non-skid
tread is all about . . . "

"It is the same on all of us," she said, "so that if any
two come together, they fit, each feature." True: the
pattern was symmetrical. With two Demu face to face,
every bump would meet a dimple. There were about a

dozen of each. Barton was too embarrassed to count carefully; it had been a long time since he'd played " . . . and I'll show you mine."

"In breeding season," Eeshta continued, "two adults come facing together and hold. From the concave parts which have the eggs, a substance flows that hardens and maintains the two tightly together but does not block the passages. From the convex parts then come cells to fertilize the eggs. The two Demu are not entirely awake but are in bliss. A day later comes the hard work of breaking loose from each other. Then the eggs are laid, each adult's into its own breeding tank. The hatching and growth cycles are complex, too long to explain now. Only a very few of many survive. Dr. Ling is writing a paper on it, I think."

"I'll try to get around to reading it."

"So for me," Eeshta concluded, "Hishtoo provided the egg, not the other cell."

Yeah, I think I've got it now, Barton thought. Hishtoo's her mommy; at the same time Hishtoo was being some other little Demu's daddy. Or several. And Whnee, or Eeshta, wasn't a "she" at all; the concept didn't apply. Nonetheless Barton continued to think of the young Demu as female.

"Well, thanks for telling me," he said finally. "I think we'd better be heading back now, don't you?" Eeshta was agreeable; they began the return walk. They had gotten well away from the building complex and were in open country; Eeshta seemed to enjoy looking around, observing the terrain. The walk back was mostly silent. Something was nagging at Barton's mind, something about Eeshta. It wouldn't come clear. Maybe more conversation would jog it loose.

"What are you going to be doing next, Eeshta?"

"I want to learn more. Much more. There is a great deal to learn, I think."

"Yeah, I wouldn't be surprised. But then what?" He really shouldn't push the kid this way, Barton thought. How can a prisoner make plans? But at least Eeshta was only a captive, not a zoo creature and experimental animal as Barton and the others had been.

"If you ever take me back to my people," Eeshta said,

"I will be a—a missionary, you call it. I will tell how you are also people and not to be treated as animals or made like Siewen or the Freak."

"That's a worthy cause," Barton said absently. Then it hit him. "Like *who?*"

"Like Siewen or the Freak," she said in puzzlement. *Siewen.* Not "Shiewen."

Barton had become so used to the *sh-zh* lopped-tongue accent of Siewen and Limila that he no longer heard it consciously. So he hadn't noticed until now what had been nagging at him—that Eeshta's pronunciation was perfect.

"Say after me, Eeshta," he said. "Siewen. Shiewen."

"Siewen. Shiewen. Why, Barton?" Then Eeshta gave the Demu smile. "Oh, I see. It's the thing they made for me. Look."

She opened her mouth wide and pointed to its roof. There was a piece of acrylic plastic there, like part of a dental plate. And it made a ridge that Eeshta's short tongue could touch squarely to make the sounds of *s* and *z*.

"Every morning I must spread a paste on it so it stays in place," she said. "The man who made it showed how to do this. A dentist, he is called."

A dentist. Dental plates. Barton, you are the most stupid man in the world.

"We'd better get on back, Eeshta. There are some things I have to do."

They walked faster then, not talking. Barton was in a hurry when he left Eeshta off at her guarded home. He took time, though, to thank the guard for letting her come walking, to gravely thank Eeshta herself for the pleasure of her company and to assure her he'd see her again soon. Eeshta gave him the Demu smile and went indoors.

Barton hotfooted it to his own quarters. As he tried to get Tarleton on the phone, he was thankful that Limila wasn't there. He didn't dare let her know what he had in mind, until he knew more. Tarleton wasn't in his office, and Barton couldn't get through to the ship; those lines were hot most of the time. He flipped a mental coin and decided to stick his neck out; he punched the number of

Dr. Arleta Fox, and got her on the third ring. He wasted no time in idle chatter.

"This is Barton. About the medical group here on the project—how are we fixed for plastic surgeons?"

It took a little time. Dr. Fox reached the ship via a priority line. Tarleton checked back to see exactly what Barton had in mind. When Barton told him, he didn't argue.

"I feel stupid as hell," Barton said, "for not thinking of this sooner. The only saving grace is that none of the rest of you bastards did, either." He could say that to Tarleton, because his real respect was no secret to either of them.

"I suppose the reason we didn't—and believe me, Barton, I feel every bit as badly about it as you do—is that we have only seen your companions as they are now."

"Yeah, I guess that's so. But hell, I don't have even that excuse."

"You had your own worries, Barton. Nice that you're working out of them."

Two days later Barton was talking with a plastic surgeon named Raymond Parr, a tall languid-seeming man, in an office not far from Dr. Fox's. They were looking at Barton's paintings of the Limila-that-had-been, alongside some unflattering closeups of Limila as she was now. "What do you think you can do, Doctor?"

Parr was in no hurry. He looked at the pictures and at the paintings. Finally he spoke. "It depends on how far you and the prospective patient are willing to go. I assume from my limited knowledge of this entire project that expense is no object. A great deal more can be done in the way of repairs, these days, than most people think. But there are limits; in some cases these depend on whether it is appearance or function that you have in mind." Dr. Parr raised his eyebrows at Barton as if he'd asked a question; Barton shrugged the ball right back to him.

"All right; let's go down the list systematically. I could add a toe to each foot with a cartilage graft, but it wouldn't bend naturally; same thing with the fingers. I'd advise you to leave all that alone, but it's your choice; it might be worth it on the feet, at that, for better balance. The nails are gone; if you like, I can recess niches for cosmetic glue-on nails. For social purposes a few well-shaped daubs

of nail polish would do nearly as well, and be less difficult and expensive." Barton shook his head with impatience,
but he was making notes.

"Well, whatever you choose," the doctor continued.
"The navel is no problem; any of my assistants as a
routine chore can remodel one or delete it or punch out
a new one in a better cosmetic location. As to the simu-
lation of external genitals, it's a simple matter to stretch
folds of skin and bond them into place, if you wish. And
I assume you'll want the minor abdominal scarification
removed."

Too bad that's not all it would take for Siewen or the
Freak, Barton thought wryly.

"Plastic insert breasts are common these days," Parr
went on, "but a padded bra would do the job nearly as
well, unless one of you is a fetichist." Parr never knew
how close he was, then, to sudden violence; Barton's
face didn't show what he felt.

Parr paused; it was a habit he had. "I realize the head
and face are your major concern, Mr. Barton." Well, about
time! "I assume you realize a wig will be needed, along
with false eyelashes and stick-on eyebrows." Barton
nodded; would this sonofabitch *ever* get to the point? "And
dentures, of course." Of course. "The tongue is beyond
my skills; amputation of muscular tissue cannot be re-
versed at this time."

But the face, you fool, you goddam fool; the *face*.

"Our remaining problems," said Parr, "and they are
the most important ones, of course, are the nose, the
ears and the lips." Barton braced himself.

"I can make her a good nose by use of cartilage grafts,
with perhaps a bit of plastic implanting if need be; the
skin will stretch and bond to it. I will not guarantee to
match your paintings exactly because these things don't
work that predictably, but I can promise you a presentable and even a handsome nose."

He hesitated. "Mr. Barton, I couldn't guarantee you
a thing about trying to restore the ears. Skin, even
grafted skin, won't stretch and bond dependably, around
the extensive concave angles that make up much of normal ear structure." Parr sighed. "I suggest you settle for
cosmetic prostheses, soft-plastic ear-cups."

Well, if it had to be . . . the wig would cover them, anyway. The *lips*, now.

"The mouth presents a real problem." Yeh, let me tell you what the problem is. Well, he would in a minute, Barton thought.

"Tissue has been cut away in sawtoothed notches at about a 45-degree angle, nearly a quarter of an inch into both upper and lower lips. The question is whether to cut back to a smooth line or try to divert some of the tissue from the tips of the serrations into the deepest part of the gaps. The one alternative would shorten facial length nearly half an inch; the other might leave wrinkles in the lips, even though we'd use stitchless bonding at the surface layers. In either case we must semi-detach and stretch some mucous membrane of the mouth's inner lining to constitute the outer visible lip tissue when the operation is complete, and this is always chancy. It might not hold, or it might contract and pull the lips inward. The least risky alternative is to cut back all the way and make do with the shortened facial structure." No, Doctor; safer than that is to hang yourself.

There was more discussion; Barton hadn't got it all straight on the first reading, and he needed to have it very straight indeed. He thanked Parr and told him he'd be in touch in a day or two. As an afterthought he asked the doctor to remove the cast from his arm; it came off like peeling a banana. Then Barton left and talked to the dentist, whose name he could never remember for more than five minutes, and to Tarleton, who gave him the full authorization he needed.

Barton was becoming accustomed to having to get authorization for things; it had taken him a while to realize that other people had to have some say-so. But with Tarleton it wasn't so bad.

Then he went home. Limila had dinner hot on the range for him; she herself was eating some kind of damn mush, as usual. Barton could have kicked himself.

"Hi, Limila," he said; she was answering him these days. "We've got some things to talk about."

"Hello, Barton. All right. You eat first, though." Her ragged mouth bent, and Barton realized she was trying to smile. She hadn't given him the Demu lifted-tongue smile since the first night they'd slept together. But only slept . . .

Barton ate; he had developed a good appetite, mostly for high-protein foods. He wasn't putting on any weight; thank Heaven for small favors.

Then he had to talk. "Limila . . . " he said, and began to tell her slowly and haltingly, starting from where he himself had started with Eeshta's pronunciation aid, all of what he and Dr. Parr had discussed.

He got only a short way into it when Limila started crying and couldn't stop. Barton said a little more, but it didn't help. He caught and held her to him; that didn't help, either. Then he got mad.

"Don't you *want* to get back more to yourself?" he shouted, holding and shaking her by the shoulders. Her soft fingertips with no nails moved on his face; instinctively, she was trying to claw him. His anger vanished; he realized she was fighting the revival of hope, that she couldn't stand to have it and lose it again. Barton could understand; he'd been through it.

He gentled her, gradually. And finally ventured speech again.

"Limila," he whispered, where her ear should have been, "won't you at least listen to what can be done and decide how much of it you want to try?" She nodded against his face.

"But not now, Barton, not tonight. It's too much to accept. I can't." They held each other tightly. But that's as far as it went, even later in bed together.

The next day they could and did talk it out. Barton worked from his notes, in order; it was the only way he could think to do it. Parr had said that even a stiff cartilage toe would help in walking balance, so Limila reluctantly agreed to have both feet chopped open again, if it might help. Not the hands, though; who needs a stiff finger? She did want Barton to find out whether a graft could minimize the unsightly jog at the wrist, where the Demu had stripped away the two fingers. Barton made a note; it was something he hadn't thought to ask.

Emphatically, Limila wanted her belly free of the simulated Demu sex-organ pattern. She didn't care about a navel one way or the other, but Barton thought she should have one so she agreed. Somehow, though, he couldn't bring himself to argue in the matter of external genitalia; it was a little too personal, or something. "Many Tilaran women," she told him, "are circumcised much this same way. It was a beauty fad of some years ago." Barton suddenly realized there was a hell of a lot he didn't know about the Tilari culture. Well, he'd never asked.

Breasts? "I don't know, Barton," she said. "Dead plastic lumps under my skin? But yet they might make my body feel better-balanced again." She cupped her hands, one at each side of the lower edge of her ribcage.

Barton laughed and gently moved her hands higher. "No, more like this, Limila. You're on Earth now. Haven't you noticed?"

Angrily she pushed his hands away. "I am a Tilari woman, Barton. I will have Tilari breasts or none at all."

"But——" he began. She shook her head, would not listen to him. "Oh well; skip it for now. You and the doc do whatever you decide between the two of you. But——" He wasn't getting anyplace, so finally he did skip it.

She nodded absently at his mention of wigs and so forth. Barton asked if she'd like to have one right away, and maybe the dentures. She shook her head.

"With this face? No, thank you, Barton. I prefer the hood and veil." Limila had added a half veil to the Demu garb, for working with humans, hiding everything but her eyes. Only at home with Barton would she show her face.

She was disappointed that nothing could be done about her tongue, but moderately cheered by Barton's reminder of the prosthesis that had corrected Eeshta's pronunciation. And she was unhappy that Dr. Parr felt he could not rebuild her ears.

"I suppose you had better have him provide the plastic ones," she said. "I do not know if you would have noticed, but my directional hearing is almost absent. The cups of the ears serve that function." Barton kicked himself again for having taken so long to think of doing anything about Limila's difficulties. Oh sure; he'd had his own problems, as Tarleton had pointed out. But was that excuse really good enough?

Her first real enthusiasm was for Parr's confidence in

his ability to recreate her nose. "Oh, Barton! That will be so wonderful. I *hate* this face, and that is a thing I hate most about it. But what about . . . ?" She touched her lips.

In a quiet voice he told her the two choices Parr had given.

She had to think about them. "If he tries to spread tissue to fill these in," she said, touching a finger to one of the harsh notches, "the result may be lumpy?" Barton nodded. "Or he must cut back, so they will be shorter."

"Yes."

"Second choice is preferable, I think," she said. "But I can talk about it more with Dr. Parr, what he thinks chances are in each case."

They left it at that. Limila was already late at the ship; engrossed in their discussion, neither had noticed the time. "Come on; I'll walk you over to the motor pool," he said. Limila put on her robe, hood, veil and sandals, found her notecase. They set out.

Jeeps were available, but no driver. Barton hadn't driven a car in eight years; it seemed like a good time to practice. He didn't have a driver's license, but he hadn't had one for the Demu spaceship, either.

The controls were different from the ones he'd known, but he figured them out without much difficulty. He and Limila arrived at the ship safely, without even a close call. They found Tarleton fuming quietly and pretending not to.

"We've hit some snags here," he said, giving them only a bare nod as greeting. "Siewen can't make head or tail of the astrogational data. Limila, your people have interstellar travel; maybe you can do better with it."

"I picked up a little of it on the trip back," said Barton. "Want me to sit in?"

"Later, maybe. Glad you came out, though; I have an item or two for you. Why don't you go on into the ship and let Kreugel fill you in? I'll be along as soon as we get this other on the road." He and Limila walked to the nearby prefab as Barton climbed into the ship.

Kreugel had blueprints and circuit drawings spread over most of the control room. "Hi, Barton," he said. "Good to see you." They shook hands.

"How's it coming?"

"Not bad, not bad at all. The theory boys are handing us some pretty weird answers, though. For instance, how long are the Demu supposed to have had space travel?"

"Oh, since about the time our ancestors left the forests and started using antelope bones for clubs, I'd guess. Why?"

"That's about what I thought," said Kreugel. "Then tell me how come, Barton—tell me how come in all that time they never improved their space drive?"

"How do you know they didn't?"

"Well, we don't really. But we think so. The thing is that the drive the Agency was working on—given a couple of clues from this ship—turned out to be a better, more efficient drive than the one the Demu have."

"Couldn't that be coincidence, or luck? If true?"

"Maybe. But now again, once the Agency got their drive working—"

"They *have* it working?"

"Yes, as of last Friday," Kreugel said, grinning. "Anyway, from nothing but static test runs, the boys came up with about sixteen different ideas for further improvements. Now what does that tell you, Barton?"

"It doesn't tell me the Demu are stupid, if that's what you mean. They are in some ways, such as their cultural inertia, but that little Eeshta is nobody's dummy."

"Not stupid, Barton. Just not inventive. You see it now?"

"I'm not sure, Kreugel. You tell me."

"The guess is that the Demu didn't invent this drive in the first place. They got it from somebody else, somehow, and just plain copied it. The same with the other stuff: the leaky no-splash floors, the sleep gun, the protective shield and all the rest of it. All it would take, Barton, would be the capture of one ship, plus a reasonable level of technology and a lot of patience. I'm told we could have done it ourselves as early as—well, whenever semiconductor application was first being developed."

"Late 1940s," Barton recalled. "Well, it's an interesting idea, but what's so important about it?"

"It means that we can build ships that outclass the

Demu—and that maybe they can't improve theirs without a model to copy."

"Hmm, maybe so," said Barton. "I wouldn't bet too
big a bundle on it, though."

Tarleton came in. "Hi. How far along are you?"

"Just that somebody thinks the Demu are copycats, not
inventors, and stole their antigravity and everything,"
said Barton. "I'm not totally sold, but it could be. What
else is there?"

"Not too much. But before you leave I'd like you to
check Limila's interpretation of the astrogational data.
She's pretty sure she's right, but you're the one who
worked with it." Barton nodded, waiting for Tarleton to
continue. Kreugel waved them off and went back to his
blueprints. The two men moved out into the other compartment.

"Kreugel tell you the Agency has its own drive working?"

"Yeah, and improved six ways from Sunday over this
one, he says. No kidding?'"

"Fact," said Tarleton. "The lab people are going out of
their minds with the possibilities. Apparently they were
only a couple of jumps from the whole anti-gravity thing
already. They have to admit that those jumps weren't in
the direction they were trying to go; they'd been on a
wrong track. But they claim it would have been a matter
of only a few months. They could be right; those lads
don't spend too much time in blind alleys."

"So what's next?" Barton was getting bored with the
Agency's ego trip.

"Well, they've cobbled together this one ship, a sort of
breadboard model, to experiment with. Washington is in
a hurry to settle on an adequate design and get into
production: the old argument between 'Get it on the
road *now*' and 'Give us a little more time so we can make
it better!'. You know."

"Afraid I can't help you much on that," Barton grinned.
"I learned a long time ago to keep my neck out of policy
arguments."

"Maybe so, but I want your advice on the auxiliary
hardware. Just how far do you think we should go in du-
plicating what the Demu carry?"

Barton shook his head impatiently. "I don't know all that much about it, Tarleton. We don't need their fancy floors; plumbing's simpler. Or the no-source lighting; it's nice to have no shadows on your control console but not necessary. I imagine those two items would be a big part of the cost problem, so skip 'em.

"When it comes to weapons, maybe I brought you the wrong ship. The bigger ones may have stuff we don't even know about, and you can bet that Hishtoo won't be telling us anything he doesn't have to. This crate has the unconsciousness weapon—the sleep gun, you call it—and the shield. Personally, I don't even know what the shield will handle and what it won't. But if there's more offense or defense on here, I never found it."

"Yes, I thought that would be about the size of it. Nobody else found anything more in the way of weapons, either. But we still haven't eliminated the possibility of another of those tricky 'Enable' switches like the one for the circuit diagrams. It's a slow cautious process, checking out *all* the comboes on that control board.

"Anyway, they're testing the shield, all right. Took a pilot model out into space on a rocket shuttle, with all sorts of test objects and instruments and telemetering equipment inside. Now they're throwing everything at it but the kitchen sink."

"Any useful results?"

"So far, the sumbidge will take anything *we* know how to throw, except for coherent radiation. That goes through it like a knife through cheese."

Barton laughed. "So we just take a big-daddy laser . . . "

"So big it takes up the whole central axis of one of our new ships . . . "

"And ZAP! Well, I hope it works."

"That makes a crowd of us. But we still have a problem."

"Let me tell you what the problem is," thought Barton. But the other man didn't say it.

"How effective is the shield against the sleep gun or vice versa?" he asked. "That's not a simple question. It's a matter of the power to the gun and the power to the shield, the distance, and the time of exposure."

"So what the hell? Test it."

"On whom, Barton? We've already used it to knock Hishtoo out once, to make sure it would work on the Demu as it does on humans. We don't dare take a chance on scrambling his memories much; we *need* the hardshelled bastard, for what information we can worm out of him."

Well, by God, there *was* a problem. It would take a lot of testing to get the necessary answers, and the sleep gun played hell with memory. Who was going to volunteer for a case of amnesia? Not Barton, for sure; he'd had that bit, and still he wasn't sure all his mental nuts and bolts were back in the right bins.

"Yeh, you've got a point. Lemme think a minute . . ."

There had to be answers; Barton thought of one. Some men and women were trapped in cages, permanently.

"The hopelessly insane, Tarleton. It's their memories that have them tied up in knots. The sleep gun might even cure a few. If it doesn't, they haven't lost a hell of a lot, have they?"

Tarleton looked dubious. "Pragmatically it makes sense, but we'll play hell trying to get authorization. A lot of people would holler bloody murder, you know."

"Federal booby hatch," said Barton. "That big one near D.C. The Agency can slap Security on the whole bucket."

"You give harsh answers, don't you? Well, it can't hurt to try, I guess. Thanks." Barton was beginning to make motions preliminary to leaving. "Oh, don't forget to check Limila on the astrogation; OK? And in a few days we'll want you to take some student pilots up in this ship. Also in the new Agency model, to show them how it goes and give us an operational comparison."

"Hell, any of your trainees could fly this thing right now."

"Yes, but they haven't done it. You have." Barton shrugged an OK, and left. Outside, he realized he hadn't said goodbye to Kreugel. Oh well; the man probably wouldn't want to be interrupted again anyway.

Over at the prefab he checked Limila's interpretation of the data necessary to travel from Star A to Star B. As he had expected, she had it right. He noticed that Hishtoo seemed distinctly wary of him; that reaction didn't hurt Barton's feelings. Siewen didn't say much, but seeing him gave Barton an idea: Maybe before working on Limila, Dr. Parr could use a trial run.

Limila wasn't needed for the rest of the day, so Barton took her with him in the jeep. He enjoyed testing its performance and handling over the bumpy dirt road, now that he had the hang of it. First he stopped by Dr. Parr's office to make sure the doctor could see Limila that afternoon. Then he and she went home for lunch and a shower; the day was hot. There was a note in the mailbox; Dr. Fox wanted to see Barton.

Dr. Parr had priority; they went to his office immediately after lunch. Although he had seen the pictures, the doctor was visibly shocked when Limila doffed the veil and hood. He hid it well but fooled no one. Quickly, though, he put his professional manner together and carefully examined Limila's head and face, hands and feet. He didn't ask her to disrobe; Barton remembered that Parr considered the problems of the torso to be minor.

"Your description and pictures were accurate, Barton," he said. "I see no reason to change the prognoses I gave you earlier. Does she wish to proceed?"

"Hell, Doctor; ask her. She's right here in front of you, brains and all." Parr colored.

"I'm sorry, madam," he said; Barton didn't bother to correct him about Limila's marital status. "It is only that . . . "

"I know," said Limila. "I cannot ever get used to it, either. That is why I hope you can help me." Her eyes filled with tears. Parr was obviously shaken.

Barton cut in to display Limila's wrists and ask if anything could be done about the jog where the fingers had been cut back.

"Either plastic sponge or cartilage could be used to fill out a smoother line," Parr said. "Cartilage would be best but we will be using quite a lot of that elsewhere; the supply is not unlimited."

"Well, however it works out," said Barton. "Look, I think I'll leave you two to work out the details. The lady shrink wants me again. See you at home, later, Limila. See you too, Doctor, and thanks." Handshake, pat her shoulder, and out.

Dr. Arleta Fox welcomed him smilingly. He noticed that her dark-red hair had been shortened a little and tamed a lot; it was nowhere near as frizzy as before. She wasn't a bad-looking little woman, Barton thought, if you liked strong jaws and didn't mind the implication of tenacity.

"We'd like to do some nonverbal tests today, Mr. Barton." You mean "you," lady; "we" don't want to do anything of the sort. But he smiled and nodded; the two of them exchanged polite bla-bla-blas on the way to the testing room.

The ceiling was low and gray, and Barton's guard went up. This woman had been reading the reports on him, *really* reading them.

But the tests weren't too bad. First there were a number of color-filled sheets of paper bearing abstract patterns. He was supposed to choose which he liked best, and least, out of a dozen or so groups of five each. Inevitably he was drawn to the gaudiest, most violent combinations and bored by the pastels; naturally he announced the opposite choices. Dr. Fox looked dubious, but didn't say anything.

Then came the good old Rohrschach ink blots: "Tell me what you see in these, and tell me a story about each one, if you can, please."

Barton saw a mutilated woman dying in mindless pain. "This is a little boy in a Hallowe'en mask. He is going out trick-or-treating."

He saw two grotesque entities ready to lock in mortal combat. "A boy and a girl are having a picnic, out in the country." The room was air-conditioned, but he was sweating worse than he'd done outdoors in the heat. Dr. Fox paid no apparent heed.

Barton saw a group of pseudo-lobsters who had once been human beings. "I get the impression of a family of baby rabbits. I guess my imagination is throwing in the ears; they sure aren't in the picture, are they?" He hoped it looked like a smile, what his face was doing on the outside. Because that had been too close.

Finally it was over and he could leave, smiling and bla-blaing with Arleta Fox. In another job, he felt, he could have liked her.

When he got home, Limila was fixing dinner. She appeared happier than he'd ever seen her, though with an undertone of anxiety.

But "Later, Barton; eat first," she said when he asked. For a girl who had never seen Earthly foodstuffs until recently, he thought (not for the first time) that she was developing into one helluva good country-style cook.

Idly he noticed a row of scratches down her right arm. Not so idly, he saw that some were red and swollen. "What's all that?"

Testing for allergy reactions to antibiotics, it turned out. Dr. Parr had no wish to resort to full-asepsis surgery if he could help it; bacteria abound, and mutate. And he wanted to begin operations the next afternoon, if possible. Starting with Siewen.

Barton nearly had to laugh when Limila told him of the Great Breast Controversy. Parr hadn't quite understood Limila's differences from Earth-human; he'd been flabbergasted when she told him where she wanted her surrogate breasts implanted. "Then he refused," she told Barton. "He said he cannot rebuild an anatomy he doesn't know. So we decided none at all, for this time. He thinks I will change my mind . . . "

But there was more, Barton could tell. And for once, he *did* want to hear what the problem was. He was a long time getting it out of her. Finally in bed, in the dark, holding each other like two small children afraid of the bogeyman, she said it.

"The pain, Barton. The pain again. I am afraid."

"Well, sure," he said, "these things hurt some, as they heal up. But it's not all that bad. I mean, it's sure as hell worth it, isn't it?"

"No, I mean the cutting, the stretching, the binding together, all of that. It was very bad before, Barton, with the Demu. Why should it be easier now?"

He sat upright, dislodging her from his embrace. "For Chrissakes! Didn't the Demu put you to sleep for all that butchering? Or even give you a shot or pill to kill the pain?"

They hadn't. The sleep gun? "They never use it again on one they have decided to make Demu. With much use, effects on memory become permanent." Barton cringed, thinking what she must have endured.

"But you don't think *we* do surgery that way? You have surgeons on Tilara; what do they use to control pain?"

"There is a drug; pain becomes ecstasy. I think you do not have it here."

"If we have, it's probably illegal. We use anesthetics; you go to sleep, and wake up when it's all over. Didn't Parr say anything?"

"No."

"Did you ask him?"

"About pain, I ask. No trouble, he said; we do it with a general. I say no. Such a foolish idea!"

"Huh? I don't get you. Run that one through again."

"A general? Like the man Parkhurst? What could he do?"

Barton broke up; he couldn't help it. Grabbing Limila and hugging her fiercely, he laughed so hard that tears came. He hadn't laughed like that in over eight years. Then he explained, gently, the difference between a general officer and a general anesthetic. When she understood, Limila managed a small laugh of her own. It was tentative, tremulous, but in the right direction. "It'll be all right," he said. "Really, it will."

He held her close until she was asleep. For a time he had little luck getting himself to sleep. He was thinking how much respect, even more than he had accorded her, Limila deserved for what she had gone through. Or Siewen, for that matter. Or even Whosits.

Next morning Barton was to take Dr. Parr to the ship, as well as Limila. At the motor pool, no one hassled him for permission about anything; they assumed he had it. From Parr's office he called the dentist; might as well have impressions made for plates as soon as possible. The height factor could be measured as soon as lip surgery was complete, but Parr had said the mouth would then be too tender for impression work.

At the ship, Tarleton was in a hurried mood. Compared to the slow bearlike man Barton had first met, he was practically a streak of lightning. "Barton," he said at once, "the new ship, up at Seattle, is ready for comparison testing; Boeing really pushed it to meet the contract. Tomorrow we take this one up there. All right?"

Barton shook his head, not in negation but to get his

bearings. Yes; all right. "OK, Tarleton; I'm ready if you are. But I want you to meet Dr. Parr, the surgeon who is going to do the job on Limila and the rest. I hope it doesn't bust your program any, but he needs Siewen and Limila for a while, starting this afternoon."

Tarleton started to swell and possibly burst like the frog in the fable, but he too shook his head and considered his priorities. "How long?" he asked. "Will I have access to them for questions if I need them?" Barton turned to Dr. Parr for the answers.

"Not for the first three days, Mr. Tarleton. Even with the newer drugs, it takes that long to reduce the swelling; it used to take weeks." He paused. "Will that be satisfactory?"

Tarleton started to speak. Then he looked at Limila, remembering what was hidden by the hood and veil. He looked at Siewen, too. "Hell, I guess I can spare three days. Considering everything. After all, I'll be busy up north that long, before I can leave Barton on his own."

It was settled. Tarleton wanted to run Hishtoo through one last intensive grilling session before he turned Siewen and Limila over to Parr. To pass the time, waiting, Barton took the latter into the ship for a guided tour and some chat with Kreugel. There wasn't much that was news to Barton, but he liked Kreugel and didn't mind hearing again what obviously interested Parr. The only new facts were the initial results of testing the sleep gun versus the shield: as expected, given the maximum of power to both, you were safe behind the shield unless you were too close to the gun for too long. The parameters were still being evaluated, but the limits had been determined. Barton didn't ask about the effects on the test subjects. He didn't really want to know.

Toward lunchtime, he and Parr bade goodbye to Kreugel and went to the prefab, to pick up Limila and Siewen. No one had asked Siewen whether he wanted to be remodeled or not; Barton because it never entered his mind, and no one else because this was Barton's personal project. Siewen had heard the proposal discussed and hadn't said anything one way or the other, but then he never did, except to answer questions. Not any more.

In the prefab were Tarleton, Limila, Hishtoo, Siewen and

two people Barton knew by sight but not by name. Assistants of some kind. He nodded to all.

"You have it about wrapped up for now, Tarleton?" he asked. The place was tense: Tarleton was obviously displeased, Limila stood in an apologetic stance. Siewen looked as if he weren't there at all, and Hishtoo looked defiant.

"What's the problem?" said Barton, and mentally kicked himself for saying it that way.

"Oh, Hishtoo's up on his high horse." Tarleton sounded weary. "He's just realized we're going to take this game back onto his own home grounds, and he doesn't like the idea."

Hishtoo suddenly shrilled a rapid burst of lobsterese. "He says," Limila interpreted, "that we animals had best not dare disturb the homes of the Demu."

"Well now, is that right?" said Barton. He knew he looked nasty; he knew he sounded nasty. Above all, he knew that he couldn't afford to show it, not before Tarleton, of all people. But he couldn't help himself. He walked up to Hishtoo, face to face. "To you I'm an animal?" he said softly. "To me, you're crab salad!"

Hishtoo cringed and turned away. "I'll be damned," Tarleton said in a hushed voice, "That hardshell understands more English than he lets on." He turned to Barton. "When I said that to him I was twisting his arm and shouting. But you said it just like 'Pass the bread' and it got to him."

"Not quite," said Barton, knowing he shouldn't. "More like 'Pass the crab salad.'" Tarleton looked at him, but said nothing more except the usual so-longs. Barton herded Parr and Siewen out to the jeep, Limila following. He agreed to meet Tarleton in the morning, and drove off.

Lunch at the Barton-Limila residence was on the awkward side. Doktor Siewen was being as nonexistent as possible. Limila's reluctance to show her face to anyone except Barton was eased somewhat because Parr had already examined it, but her discomfort was apparent. Parr's appetite was scanty for a man of his size; the reasons were obvious. Barton ate like a horse and complimented Limila on her cooking; it was one of his days to be contrary (though the food *was* good).

Next stop, he announced, was the dentist. No, come to think of it, first they would drop by and pick up Whosits; Barton hadn't seen him for weeks and hadn't missed him, but the Freak could also benefit by a set of dentures, so that he wouldn't have to subsist on mushy gloop all his life. So what the hell . . .

The guard at the door of the unit housing Siewen, Whosits and the two Demu accepted Barton's authorization readily enough. Eeshta was pleased to see Barton; he expressed his own pleasure at seeing her. Whosits was something else again. He didn't want to go anywhere. Barton and Parr took him out the hard way but not very; Whosits was so flabby as to be wholly ineffectual.

The dentist was noticeably jolted by the looks of his patients, but he took Limila's and Siewen's dental-plate impressions with reasonable aplomb. Whosits made a problem of himself; he refused to open his mouth. Dr. Parr explained the purpose of the project, but Whosits paid no heed. Barton took over then, not gently. Whosits not only opened his mouth but then also kept it closed—on the second try—for the proper length of time to produce a usable impression. Meanwhile Parr was explaining how he was going to help Whosits look presentable once more in human society. He was working with a tough audience.

As soon as the hardened impression was removed, Whosits reared back and spoke words. Actual human words, the first Barton had ever heard from him.

"Nein; nein! Ich bin Demu! DEMU; Hören Sie?"

Barton shook out his rusty knowledge of German and tried to talk with the creature, but that was all Whosits would say. "Oh, the hell with it," Barton said, finally. "If this nut wants to stay a lobster, why argue with him?" Parr said nothing. He did not object when Barton dumped the Freak back at his own guarded quarters, before the rest of the group went on to Parr's office and improvised operating room.

(Later, through hush-hush channels, Whosits' fingerprints turned out to be those of one Ernst Heimbach, missing from East Berlin for about five years. Barton suggested, "Why don't we dump him back where he belongs?" but Tarleton said, "Hell, if we did, they'd blame his condition on *us*." The old Cold War had softened into almost-free

trade, considerable real cooperation and very little risk
of hot war, Barton learned, but somehow the propaganda
part continued as idiotic and irritating as ever.)

Parr summoned a couple of nurses to take charge of
Limila and Siewen for the preliminaries; Barton was about
to become superfluous. He took Limila in his arms, pushed
her hood back enough to kiss her forehead. "I'll see you
in a few days," he said, "when I get back from Seattle."
She nodded but said nothing. "Look now. I'd be around
with you if I could; you know that. But Tarleton wants
those test runs in a hurry and I'm tagged for it. You'll be
all right; Parr is *good.* And I'll see you, soon as I can."

"All right, Barton," she said, finally. "I hope then you
can like what you see." She turned abruptly and followed
a nurse out of the office, not looking back. Siewen and the
other nurse trailed after.

Barton looked at Parr. "I know you'll do what you can."

"I'll try to do better than that, Barton. You know?
The hardest thing to realize in this case—please don't
take offense—is that I should be seeing her as a woman
to *restore.* Forgive me, but I've been seeing a *something*
to be turned into a woman."

Barton sighed, not angry. "Yes, Doctor; I know how it
must be for you." They shook hands. "However it works
out, be kind to her."

Barton went home to be alone with himself and his
memories. It wasn't fun. He skipped dinner and got drunk.
Not too drunk; he went to bed at a reasonable hour. Alone,
and missing Limila more than he would have thought
possible.

Knowing that Tarleton, next morning, would be like a
cat on a hot stove, Barton got up early. He breakfasted
quickly and with his packed suitcase was at the ship a few
minutes ahead of the other man. Three of the four student-
pilots were there before him; the fourth arrived almost on
Tarleton's heels.

Tarleton cut into the exchange of greetings. "All right,
we're here. Let's get on board and stash our luggage." They
did so quickly, and followed Barton into the control area.

The room normally seated two. Tarleton had had four
more seats installed for training purposes. Even though

these were small, bucket-type shells, the seating was cramped. But they all wedged in; no one complained. Well, they'd better not have, with Tarleton on edge as he was.

Barton explained the major controls. "I won't bother running you through the whole switch panel because ours are different, they tell me; our people left out a lot of things on here that we won't really be needing, so as to get into production sooner.

"The principles will be the same. Start out with all the small toggles off and your guidance lever *here* and go-pedal *here*, both in neutral; then you apply power with this blue jobbie in the middle." He knew they'd heard the instructions before but it didn't hurt to tell them again, and at the same time reinforce his own knowledge. "All right, here's your outside viewscreen and here's your 'Drive on' switch," pointing them out, throwing them and remembering how in the Demu aircar he'd discovered them in reverse order. What a panic *that* had been. "Artificial gravity, indoors here, set to hold at one-G. Now we're hot to trot; here goes nothing." And he took the ship up.

He took it straight up at maximum lift, because he wanted them to realize immediately the kind of power they'd be handling. At an altitude of about one thousand kilometers he made the tightest right-angle turn the ship would manage, pointing out the rather incredible G-forces that, because of the artificial gravity field, they were *not* feeling. Then he slowed to roughly orbital-drift speed, put the major controls to neutral, and clambered out of the pilot's seat.

"OK, I want each of you to play around with this can for a while, out here where it's safe. You first, Kranz." Kranz climbed gingerly into Barton's pilot chair; Barton squeezed into the empty one. "For now," Barton continued, "we work only with the two drive-control levers; leave all the little toggles alone unless I tell you different. And don't use more than half power. Just play loose in this general volume of space. OK?"

Each man had about a half-hour of practice, mostly experimenting on his own with only an occasional suggestion from Barton. Kranz started cautiously and gradually built up his confidence. Slobodna, the next man, did the opposite, applying all his allowed half power immediately in violent maneuvers, losing orientation and scaring himself. But then, after a few minutes of more cautiously feeling out the controls, he too achieved a degree of mastery over them. The other two, Jones and Dupree, began with medium-power settings and modest acrobatics; each progressed to as proficient a handling of the craft as could be expected in so short a time. Barton was satisfied with the lot of them.

"OK, Dupree; that's fine," he said. "I might as well get back in the saddle now, and take us down. My gut says it must be nearly time for lunch."

"Just a minute." It was Tarleton.

"What's the problem? Aren't you hungry yet?"

"Damn it, Barton! Don't you think *I* want a turn at driving this kiddie car?"

Barton laughed; hell, he should have thought of that. "OK, Tarleton, she's all yours."

Tarleton was a model of caution and precision. He never applied the maximum-agreed power nor made violent rolls or turns. He returned the ship quite closely to his starting point and to drift speed before turning it over to Barton.

"Thanks, Barton. I just wanted to fly a spaceship once in my life. You realize that once the program is under way, an unqualified guy like me won't have a chance."

"Hell, you can fly any ship *I* have any say-so about, any time you want." Tarleton was silent; finally Barton realized why. He, Barton, probably wasn't going to *have* any say-so about these things much longer, is what it meant. Well, maybe. People had had that kind of attitude about Barton before. Like the Demu, for instance. Barton filed the whole bit for future reference. After all, it wasn't as though he'd failed to provide for the contingency.

"OK, gang," he said. "I'm going to haul her down like a real bat, so you can see how she hits air. Then I'll ease her back, just above SST traffic levels, and go in quiet from there." He chuckled. "It's going to be fun trying our own ship; from what I hear, it has considerably more legs on it than this baby has."

He took her down like a real bat indeed; his passengers,

including Tarleton, were noticeably shaken. Barton chuckled to himself, thinking how they might have reacted to his first atmospheric entrance, when he'd guessed wrong and nearly joined the Submarine Service before he pulled out of his dive. He decided not to mention that occasion.

He flipped a jury-rigged switch for the special channel to Boeing Field; Control gave him the OK to drop in on a straight vertical. He made a good landing because the Demu shield allowed no other kind. He wondered if, later, everyone shouldn't learn to land without the shield, just in case.

Barton had heard that it always rained in Seattle, but the six of them stepped out to face a sunny day. Claeburn, the Space Agency's liaison man, apologized for the unusual heat wave—all of 80 degrees. After New Mexico it felt like a cool pleasant early-morning. In fact, the time was a little after noon; they had lunch at a nearby restaurant. Claeburn suggested the company cafeteria but Tarleton wanted a drink with his lunch, and insisted. Barton was damn glad; he wanted one too. He was appalled at the size of the luncheon check picked up by Claeburn. Inflation hadn't slowed down.

After a briefing so lengthy that the drinks had had plenty of time to wear off, Barton put the prototype, Earth's first starship, through its paces. It carried about 50 percent greater acceleration than the Demu version, nearly as much advantage on tight turns, and an interlock that would not allow hard maneuvering to overload and blow the ship's internal gravity field. Barton hadn't known, and was surprised enough to say so, that such a danger existed on the Demu ship; apparently he had been wildly lucky not to exceed the limit. Especially, he thought, on his first re-entry to Earth. He felt uncomfortable, having his ignorance exposed. He felt it put more chinks in his image than he really needed.

The revised controls were no problem. There were about two-thirds as many toggles as in the Demu ship—larger, more widely spaced, and each clearly labeled. Claeburn had run them through the list of functions, anyway; it couldn't hurt. Barton could see that pilot training was going to be a real snap, especially after the four trainees, Tarleton and even Claeburn had given the new ship a workout. The procedure was like that of the morning try-outs, but faster and smoother. And more comfortable: the seats weren't so crowded. Barton felt that they were definitely making progress.

Over dinner, just the two of them, Tarleton explained the Agency's plans. "Tomorrow and the next day, you take those four men up and wring them out on navigation, test procedures and trouble-shooting; stuff like that. Pilot practice is incidental at this stage, but they'll be getting it, anyway. Mainly, though, you're training the next generation of instructors."

"Jeez," Barton protested, "I don't know any more about testing and trouble-shooting than they do."

"But they think you do," Tarleton answered. "Here are the books; you and I can go over them tonight. I've skimmed them; they're well put together, easy to follow. All you have to do is keep two jumps ahead of those four guys for the next few days. Then you come on back south in the Demu ship and they're on their own."

"But why me?" Barton was sincerely puzzled. "Why not the guys who *wrote* the books?"

"Because you are the one man on Earth who has actually piloted an interstellar trip. I know and you know how much luck you needed, but you have no idea how much the simple fact means to the Agency. They think you're Superman. It's simpler to let them keep thinking so, because then when you pass your students as trained they'll figure some of it rubbed off. You see?"

Barton saw. He saw, moreover, how maybe it gave him a handle on something he wanted, something he was utterly damn well going to have.

"Tarleton," he said, "if I'm all that important, how about letting me in on the Top-Hush? I mean, we're building ships and training pilots. What are we going to do with them?"

Tarleton was quiet for a time. "All right, Barton," he said finally. "I guess you deserve to know. Most of it, anyway.

"We're having forty ships built, all about the same as the one we flew today, but more advanced. You noticed ours is somewhat bigger than the Demu ship, to carry the more powerful drive. The hulls and loose hardware have been in production since the second week after you got home. I've put in the OK to go ahead and standardize on the drive units as-is, based on our tests today; the theory boys can incorporate later improvements into our second fleet, and so on. And what we're going to do should be obvious. We're going after the Demu."

"We?" said Barton, very quietly.

"Well, not you or I personally, of course. After all—"

"The hell you say!" Barton hadn't meant to put it like that, but there it was. "Me personally! Very definitely, me personally. Who the hell's fight do they think this is, anyway?"

"Well, I know how you must feel, of course, but you can't really expect the Agency and the military to let an outsider into the act, can you?"

"I can," said Barton. "I can and I do. You think I can't?" Slowly, deliberately, he pushed the stack of training books off the table; they landed on the floor in disarray. He looked Tarleton in the eyes, both of them suddenly quiet.

"You want me to pick those books up, Tarleton?"

After a while, Tarleton nodded slowly. Barton picked up the books, dusted them off, stacked them neatly. "All right, Barton, you've made your point. I'll do the best I can for you."

"You'll get me one of those ships. In charge of it."

"I'll try."

"You'll *do* it." He leaned forward across the table. "Listen, Tarleton, I can do a lot more for you, than be some sort of lousy figurehead. You say we're going after the Demu. Just like that?"

"Just like that."

"That's stupid. You know how big they are? I don't either, for sure, but I do know a little, from what Limila learned. I told it, but maybe nobody paid attention.

"They inhabit—that's *inhabit*—about a dozen planets. To our one. On top of that they have 'farm planets' with a few Demu supervising populations of ready-made Demu like Limila and Whosits—but of many races, not only humanoid. They have those poor bastards brainwashed into altering their own children to the Demu style of looks. Then they have research stations like the one I was at, the one that had never seen humanoids before. There were six ships at that station alone, until I stole one. Three of them hadn't been used for a while, by the looks of them, but they were there. And you're going after the Demu with a lousy forty ships?"

"What else can we do?"

"Unite and conquer, for Chrissakes! Limila's people, the Tilari, have star travel. All they don't have is the shield against the sleep gun, or any idea how to find the Demu. We can give them both."

"Well, yes," said Tarleton. "I'll put through a memo up-stairs in the Agency, on that idea. You give me the location of the Tilari planets and—"

"Limila will give you that stuff when the expedition is in space, no sooner. Christ on a crutch, you think I trust a bunch of Agency wheels to keep the faith for you? No sale. I'll go ahead with this training jazz, on your word to go to bat for me. But the Agency gets the scoop on the Tilari—and how to find the other races they know who'll want to get into the act and could help a lot—you get all that when we're on our way, not before." He wasn't bluff-ing. He'd talked the matter over with Limila; she was in full agreement with him.

"It might work, Barton." Tarleton spoke slowly. "But how do you know the Agency couldn't get the information directly from Hishtoo?"

"If Limila doesn't feel like interpreting for you? How much do you trust Siewen's abilities any more? Even if Hishtoo just happened to be feeling cooperative, which I doubt. Think about it."

Tarleton, from the looks of him, did think about it. "I think you've got us boxed, Barton. And you know some-thing? I'm glad of it. Because as you say, it is your fight." Barton looked at him and felt he could trust the big man. He purely hoped so.

The training went about as planned. On Barton's fourth day at Seattle, after seeing Tarleton off to New Mexico by SST, he was riding supercargo observing one of his first four students instructing a new batch of trainees. Three days later he decided the program had become self-sustain-ing as scheduled, and packed his suitcase. He had lunch with Claeburn and the four original trainees, enjoying this goodbye scene a lot more than he had expected. About an hour later he lifted the Demu ship off for New Mexico.

Just for the hell of it he got clearance to go by way of Luna. He cruised slowly back and forth above the surface at eyeball range, seeing the manmade installations and the undisturbed areas that had thrilled him on TV in his younger days, when the first landings had been made. With a sigh for his younger self, Barton turned back to Earth.

It took him a little time to locate New Mexico and get talked in, but eventually he found the proper spot and set the ship down. Tarleton had left the site for the day. Barton got a ride to his quarters. He called Parr and got no answer, so he had a shower before preparing a pre-packaged dinner and eating it. The package was nationally advertised over tri-V and tasted like it, but Barton hardly noticed. He was too busy being lonesome.

He called Parr again; for a wonder he got him on the first try. He could, Parr told him, see Limila the next day. In fact, the timing was good; the bandages were to be removed tomorrow. Maybe she could use Barton's presence in support. Barton tried to ask detailed questions but was brushed off. "Come see for yourself," was how Parr put it. Barton growled his thanks and hung up.

He was still restless; tomorrow was a long time away. There had been a day-old note in the mailbox: Arleta Fox was in urgent need of his company. Barton was in no hurry for that interview. He supposed he'd have to give the lady one more session of brainpicking at least, before he got the hell off Earth again. But the later the better. He was too close to making it, to take any more chances than he could help.

Now in the early evening, he decided to walk off his tensions, out in the clear air. He thought to look in on Eeshta, realizing that he hadn't had a real visit with her since the time she'd given him the clue to Limila's plight. Limila! It was going to be a long night.

The guard was unfamiliar but recognized Barton's name. "Do you want to go in, sir?" he asked.

"See if she'd like to come out for a little walk," Barton said. "We'll be back before dark. It's OK with Tarleton." The guard nodded and went inside.

Sooner than Barton expected, the guard came back with

Eeshta. She was wearing a small cap and short sleeveless robe, and sandals. Looking more acclimated all the time, Barton thought. He was surprised at the glow of real pleasure he felt at seeing her. "Hello, Eeshta," he said. "How's it going with you?"

She Demu-smiled at him. "I am happier now, Barton," she said. They strolled westward into the after-sunset light. "I learn much about your people. They are so different. Not only from ours, but from each other. It is very new and very challenging, to try to understand. I try to tell Hishtoo, my egg-parent, but he does not want to hear. He says I am becoming an animal." She hissed—the equivalent, Barton knew, of a sigh. "Perhaps one day he will be willing to learn." Barton decided he wouldn't bet much of a bundle on that possibility.

"How's the Freak doing, these days?" he said.

"Heimbach? I do not know. They took him away several days ago. I have not seen him since." Barton was faintly surprised that Eeshta knew Whosits' real name.

"Who took him?" Not that Barton cared, particularly, but it was something to say, to keep her talking.

"The man Tarleton and others I do not know." Tarleton hadn't *said* anything . . . Well, what did it matter?

"What else are you learning, Eeshta? Anything you especially enjoy?"

"Oh, yes, Barton! Your music. It is so different from ours. Some of it, I am told, is out of my range of hearing. But it seems I hear parts you do not. I think if I stay here, music will be my study and work. I like it so very much."

Barton was no music buff himself, but he asked Eeshta about her favorite composers and performers. He didn't give a damn what they discussed; he simply wanted the young Demu to feel comfortable with him. He realized he might still be feeling guilt for having roughed her up so much at first acquaintance. But the way it felt to Barton, he liked the kid, was all.

As the conversation hit a lull, it struck him that Eeshta might not know what she and her little speech-prosthesis had done, inadvertently, for Limila. So, as best he could, he tried to explain what had happened, what was being done.

"They make her as she was? It seems not to be possible. But so good, if true."

"Well, not exactly the way she was," Barton admitted, "but a lot closer. Some things, like the teeth, will be artificial. But for the most part we hope she'll look pretty much like the original model, or at least a close relative.

"The doctor is doing some work on Siewen, too," he added. "What he can."

"Poor Siewen," Eeshta said. "Some things are not possible for him, too late. And Heimbach?"

"The Freak wouldn't have any part of it, not even teeth. I guess he *likes* eating mush all the time."

"I feel badly, Barton. For Heimbach, for Siewen and Limila, for all the dead ones where we made worse mistakes. But now for Limila, and some for Siewen, I can feel better. For helping, even not knowing I helped."

"Well, you know now, Eeshta. And we're grateful to you, believe me."

"Of that, I can be glad."

The short twilight was ending. Barton took Eeshta's hand; they jogged back toward her quarters, laughing as they ran out of breath from the unaccustomed exercise. At least Barton was laughing; Eeshta's mouth was doing something he couldn't make out in the dim light, but he felt she shared his mood. Then they were home.

Her home, at least, such as it was. He started to say goodnight but Eeshta spoke first. "Barton," she said, "soon you go seeking the Demu, my people? I have heard it. It is supposed to be secret from me. But many do not believe I understand your speech. They speak where I hear, though they should not."

Barton nodded. "Yes, we have to visit the Demu at home. You can see that."

"I must go with you."

"You want to go home? Yes; sure you would. But this trip won't be too safe, you know. You'd better wait a while."

"No, *now*, Barton," said Eeshta. "I know; you will fight. With the ships. You must. Demu will not talk with what they think animals. You will force them. But I must be there, when first there is talk."

Barton didn't argue; she was right. But would Tarleton agree?

"I'll see what I can do, Eeshta." His arms acted without his volition. It was only after Eeshta had entered her quarters, and he was walking away toward his own, that Barton thought, "Well, I'll be go to hell if I didn't *hug* that hard-shelled little crittur!" Somehow it didn't bother him any.

Barton barged into his own quarters, shucked his shirt and shoes, and poured himself a hefty slug of bourbon. He looked, and carefully poured half of it back into the bottle. He sat, and sipped, and thought a lot. He went to bed early, and slept much better than he had expected.

Dr. Parr the next morning, tall, languid and about to get a flat nose if he didn't take Barton off the hook pretty soon, was in no hurry. "The patients will be with us shortly," he said. "Meanwhile let me explain some of the problems." Yeh, let me tell you what the problem is.

The trouble was that Parr told it in medicalese, which might as well have been Greek. Finally Barton had had it. "Goddammit, Doc! Did it work, or not?"

"See for yourself." Parr pushed a button on his desk; shortly, three wheelchair patients were brought in. Three?

All were wearing loose hospital-type bathrobes. Two were bald; the third had a towel around its head, bandages covering its face, and five toes on each foot. That one had to be Limila, but Barton knew Parr was going to run the show his own way. So he took a deep breath, and hoped for more patience than he could reasonably expect to have on tap.

The first chair carried a tall skinny guy who didn't look especially familiar. A little, maybe, but not much. "Say hello to Mr. Barton," said Parr.

"Hello, Barton. I am Siewen; remember?"

It wasn't, really, but there were lips and a nose, and dentures that beat the Demu accent. The ears, Barton supposed, were plastic. But what the hell.

"Hello, Doktor Siewen," Barton said. "How do you feel?" Feeling very unrealistic, himself. How long could he keep up this charade? How long could Limila?

"Much better, thank you," said Siewen. "It is good to be able to chew food again. And to pronounce correctly."

Well, good on you, Buster, Barton thought, turning to the second wheelchair. The man was no one Barton remembered.

"Who's this?" he asked Parr.

"Heimbach, of course."

"I thought he wouldn't play ball."

"Mr. Tarleton requisitioned him for tests of the Demu shield versus the sleep gun. After the third test, Herr Heimbach rediscovered the desire to be human rather than Demu." Dr. Parr grinned. "As it happens, I was able to improve things somewhat, that are not visible through the bathrobe." Barton thought he should probably feel glad for Heimbach, but he couldn't seem to find time for it.

He shook his head, hard. The formal touch, he supposed, was required.

"That's fine, Doctor," he said. "It has been interesting seeing your success with Doktor Siewen and Herr Heimbach. May we excuse them now, please?"

Parr nodded. The two were wheeled out. Barton was left alone with Dr. Parr and Limila. He walked over to her, and for the first time she looked up at him. Then she stood, and was in Barton's arms. For a moment they only held each other. Then, unsatisfactorily through the gap in the bandages, he kissed her, very gently.

The rest of it still took a while. Dr. Parr fussed about the unprofessional aspects of the reunion until Barton told him, not politely, to get on with it. Then the bandages came off, along with the towel. Not the robe, though.

The nose and lips were not quite the originals; Barton had known better than to expect perfection, though the nose was very close to it. But below the bare scalp and the fake brows and lashes was a human face. Barton found it comely and knew he could find it lovely, given the chance. The few hairline scars had already begun to fade; they would not be noticeable. He looked at Limila's new lips and was thankful for the existence of Dr. Parr, for they were close to what he had remembered. Only a little shorter.

Limila wasn't happy with the dentures; they were comfortable enough, and effective, but she wanted her full forty teeth, not merely the human twenty-eight. But she was glad to have the little ridge, so that she no longer talked like a comic drunk; Barton figured she'd settle for the rest of it eventually. He noticed that she hadn't yet bothered with simulated nails on toes or fingers, though recesses had been made for them.

The soft plastic ear-cups, part plug-in and part glue-on, were so realistic that Barton first thought they were real. Then he noticed they were cooler to the touch than real ears. Well, he could live with them if she could.

He wasn't going to ask about anything under the bathrobe, but she told him anyway. No breasts; from a quick study of dress styles she was resigned to wearing Earth-type falsies in company, but bedammt if she'd have them implanted permanently on her Tilari body. All right . . .

She confessed that she had allowed Parr to restore the appearance of external genitals, as well as the navel. "When I found it really didn't hurt," she said, "it might as well be as much the way you would like, as could be done."

Barton hugged and kissed her a lot longer than Parr appreciated, before he allowed the doctor to throw him out. He went home with more of a load off his mind than he had expected, and hardly noticed what his pre-packaged lunch didn't taste like.

In the afternoon he took a jeep and went shopping in the nearest medium-sized town, about eighty kilometers to the southwest. He had dinner there, and drove back in the evening. That night he slept without chemical aids of any kind.

The next morning, up early, it took Barton so long to reach Dr. Parr's office, by phone, that he could have walked there and saved time. He was told that he could not see Limila again immediately; Parr was running final postoperative checks on her. *But,* if he would come over around three in the afternoon, Parr finally got across through Barton's protests, he could probably bring Limila home. If the tests turned out all right. Barton thanked him sheepishly and hung up.

He decided to visit the ship; he had nothing else he wanted to do. As he started out the door, the phone rang. It was Dr. Fox.

"I'd like to see you this morning, Mr. Barton."

"Well, I was just going out to the ship."

"I spoke to Mr. Tarleton, there, and he tells me he won't

be needing you today. So why don't you come here instead? Nine o'clock?" He had to agree, he guessed, so he did.

Seated across the desk from Arleta Fox, Barton wondered at the tenacity with which this small woman dug for the worms in the undersoil of his mind. She was smiling but he didn't trust it.

After the usual perfunctory chatter, she said, "I understand that Dr. Parr's corrective surgery on your companions has been remarkably successful."

Barton nodded.

"Do you suppose the woman—Limila?—might consent to taking a few evaluative tests now?" Limila had refused anything of the sort, earlier, and the Agency (meaning Tarleton) didn't see that it had any right or authority to try to coerce her.

"I don't know; I'll ask her, if you like. But what do you expect to learn that she hasn't already told the biological and cultural teams?"

"Why, a million things! She's the first person we've met of a whole new race. If we're going to have contact with them, and I assume we are, we need to know something of what they are like psychologically, as individuals."

"Do you think she'll be typical, after what she's been through?" Then he could have kicked himself. Why remind the doctor that Barton had been through a few atypical experiences himself?

"Given a little time to stabilize, now that her appearance has been restored, I think she can give us a valid picture of what the Tilari are like. I wish she had been willing to cooperate before; the comparison would be very informative. Well, at least I can extrapolate after retesting Siewen and Heimbach."

"You've tested them?" He shook his head incredulously. "What did you find out?" Yes, lady, let's talk about somebody else, everybody else. Anybody but Barton.

"Doktor Siewen, as you probably know, seems to be devoid of normal motivations. It remains to be seen whether his change in appearance will reactivate him to any significant extent. I had little time to work with Heimback between his reversion to human speech and the beginning of the surgery by Dr. Parr; he is a very confused man. I realize that he was semi-amnesiac for a time from the results of the so-called sleep gun, but my feeling is that Heimbach has a very weak ego." She paused. "Quite different from yourself, for instance, Mr. Barton. Quite, quite different."

"Oh, hey, Doctor," Barton stammered. "Am I all that much of an egomaniac, in your book?" *Watch it, Barton; watch it!*

"A strong ego is not the same thing as egotism, Mr. Barton. I mean that unlike Heimbach you have a strong, even a fierce sense of your own individuality; it is of central importance to you. And you have a very powerful will to survive."

"That's what the tests say?" *So he hadn't fooled her much, after all.*

"I didn't need the tests to tell me that; your report of the eight years with the Demu was enough. The tests, in fact, have been unsatisfactory because they do *not* show me the man who could do what you obviously did."

Barton felt that he was in over his head. "Well, we all know a person can do more than he thinks he can, when he has to. Maybe it's just that I was under a lot of stress there, and back home here I can let down and relax." *Like hell he could!*

"Possibly. Another thought is that due to repeated exposure to the Demu sleep gun you still may have been partly amnesiac when you first took the personality tests."

"But I took the IQ tests at the same time: just before, actually. And you said they read about the same as what was already on file for me."

"Well, as I say, I'm not sure yet. So that is why I'd like you to retake the personality tests series now, Mr. Barton, if you would."

When in doubt, stall! "I really wouldn't have time for all that today, Doctor. Early this afternoon I'm supposed to pick Limila up at Dr. Parr's; he thinks she can come home now."

"I didn't mean the entire series, Mr. Barton," she said. "A few key sections: a couple of hours at most. And it's only nine-thirty . . . "

He was hooked. He knew he couldn't get away with hallucinating his younger self again to answer all the questions; for one thing it would look fishy if he asked for full privacy a second time. Well, maybe he could hallucinate a little of it now and then, without her noticing. Throw a modicum of confusion into the works. Unless she were more devious than he suspected—and he suspected one hell of a lot, where Arleta Fox was concerned—by now he had her fooled into thinking he was sane, safe to be at large. All he needed to do, probably, was soft-pedal himself on the parts he couldn't hallucinate.

She brought out the test forms—Form B, so his answers from last time would have done him no good even if he could have remembered them—and he sat down. He wasn't directly under her eagle eye, but she could look him over any time she wished, while he couldn't look to see if *she* were looking without being conspicuous about it.

He did the first few questions straight, then tried to dredge the younger Barton up to answer the next few. *He couldn't do it.* Whether it was her presence or whether he'd simply lost the knack, he didn't know. He hadn't practiced self-hypnosis since his escape; maybe that was the answer. But one way or another, he was stuck with his present self and its attitudes, to cope with a lot of tricky questions.

All right; the hell with it. Tarleton needed the help of the Tilari and other races. He couldn't get it without Limila's cooperation; in effect, that meant Barton's. Even if this lady does catch me out, he thought, she still works for Tarleton. He kept telling himself that, trying to believe it.

Finally he was done. Sweat from his armpits ran down his sides. He took the finished sheets to Arleta Fox, who did not look up until he laid the papers before her.

"All completed, Mr. Barton?"

"Best I can do, Doctor."

She pressed a button; a girl came in to take the test sheets. Presumably for scoring: no reason the doc should do all that routine guff. The girl had gone before Barton realized he hadn't noticed what she looked like—whether she was pretty or not. That wasn't like him.

"Would you like a cup of coffee before you go, Mr. Barton? I would have offered you some before, but I didn't want to interrupt your concentration."

"Yeh, sure; thanks." He sat across from her. He didn't want coffee; he wanted a drink, and to get out of here. But best to play along, just now.

The girl returned, bringing coffee. This time Barton noticed that she was slim and pretty, with blond hair cut considerably shorter than he would have preferred. Well, at least she could grow it if she wanted to, he thought with a pang, thinking how nice it would be if Limila had the same option.

"Do you have any idea when the expedition is leaving, Mr. Barton?"

Barton looked at her. Not the old security-leak ploy, for Chrissakes!

"Oh, we all know about it. But you don't have to tell me anything Mr. Tarleton told you not to. I merely wanted to get some idea of when I should cut off research and turn in my reports. They always tell me, officially, about twenty-four hours ahead of deadline. Then I don't get any sleep for a while until the reports are completed."

"Always?"

"I do research for a lot of things, Mr. Barton. This does happen to be the first interstellar expedition I've prepped for; yes." It was a wry smile, the one she gave him then.

"I don't really know, Doctor," he said. "I was up at Seattle for a week, got back yesterday afternoon. No; day before, it was. Anyway, I haven't seen Tarleton since he left Seattle, and the last I heard there was no firm date set. Or if there was, he didn't tell me."

"You don't need to sound so defensive, Mr. Barton; I believe you. More coffee?"

"No, thanks; I'd better be going. Thanks, though." He got up, they said goodbyes and he left. He wished that either he didn't feel so much like liking Arleta Fox or that he had less cause to be wary of her. His feeling for her was not sexual. Oh, he considered her attractive enough; Barton had no prejudice against small sturdy women. But what grabbed him about her was the compact tidy bulldog mind that the fierce little jaw so strongly implied. Too bad it made her such a danger to him.

Barton didn't feel like heating another frozen lunch, to eat alone. He got a jeep from the motor pool and drove out to the ship area. He caught Tarleton and Kreugel on their way to the new cafeteria. It had been established in a big hurry when Tarleton got tired of bringing his own lunch in a paper bag.

"Wait up for another hungry man, will you?" Barton called, and they did.

Inside, they went through the line and soon were sitting with laden trays. Barton didn't talk much. He was thinking of how to ask for what he wanted. Tarleton was telling Kreugel that the first ship of the Earth-built fleet would be here for testing tomorrow or the next day. Kreugel would be installing the central-axis laser weaponry.

Then Tarleton noticed Barton's silence. "What are you chewing on, over there?"

"Beef Stroganoff, it says on the menu. And a couple of questions."

"I thought the Stroganoff was pretty good, myself. Shoot the questions."

"OK," said Barton. "First, do you have any kind of proposed takeoff date yet?"

"For the fleet? Sure."

"Do I qualify to know it?"

"You're specifically authorized, I'm happy to say. Just four weeks from now, Saturday the 12th, with a possible week's slippage. OK?"

"That's pretty fast, isn't it?"

"Things get done fast on crash-priority," Tarleton said. "I haven't been just standing around here cracking whips, Barton. As soon as any item, any part of the ships is cleared for production, I start it through the line. For instance, a lot of the drive components were firm several weeks ago. I goofed on a couple and had to have them done over again when new improvements were suggested, but the waste was minor for a job of this magnitude. Before I left Seattle I put the go-ahead on the last remaining components. Production and testing is seven days a week, twenty-four hours a day: overtime and bonuses for the working troops all the way down the line. My guess is, two-to-one we don't need that extra week. OK?"

"Damn good, Tarleton. You really know how to run a railroad." He hesitated. "Now I want to ask a favor."

"Ask ahead," said Tarleton. "You have a couple coming, assuming they're reasonable."

"OK. I expect you want Limila to check over whatever your amateur translators have been getting from Hishtoo lately. And maybe you'd like me to sit in at first while your boys check out our first production-line ship. Right?"

"Yes," Tarleton agreed, "I did have those things in mind. So what's the favor?"

"Limila comes home this afternoon, I think," Barton said. "She and I can work with you tomorrow and the next day, no sweat—one or two more if you need it. But then—Tarleton, I want to take her on vacation. Show her the country; be a couple of tourists. Get lost from here—see the sights and meet the people. She needs it, you know, if she's going to be able to give her people any idea of what we're really like. I mean, a project site doesn't give much of a true picture, does it?"

Tarleton was silent for a moment. Barton could sense the wheels going around, in that brain he had learned to respect more than a little. "Dammit, Barton," he said finally, "you're right. I should have thought of that. I guess I'm too wound up in production schedules. Fair enough; you and Limila hit here bright and early tomorrow, and I won't keep you a day longer than I have to. You'd better see the Finance Office today if you can, and put in for expense money for your tour. Those people can't put a stamp on a letter in less than forty-eight hours." Barton grinned; he knew about that.

Kreugel hadn't said much but he shook hands and said "Good luck" when Barton stood up to go. "Remind me to show you how our zap-gun works when you get back."

"Yeh, I want to see that. OK, be seeing y'all."

Barton did stop at the Finance Office on his way home; he had plenty of time. A Mr. Will Groundley was querulous and resentful that Barton should want anything outside the routine. Barton's patience lasted quick, as the saying goes.

"Look," he said, "call Tarleton. He'll tell you yes or no, and then you do it or you don't. But don't quote me any more Goddam regulations, Groundley. We both know you can find something in your books to let you do anything you want, or keep you from doing anything you don't want. So get off the pot. Either you have the money here for me tomorrow, or Tarleton will find me somebody who will."

He didn't wait for an answer; one more word might have exceeded the limits of his control. He walked out and went home. For a change there were no notes in his mailbox. That was nice.

Before heading for Dr. Parr's, Barton unwrapped the results of his yesterday's shopping trip. Jeez, he hoped Limila would like them. He ran his fingers through the one he liked best . . .

Parr was not as infuriatingly languid as usual. He seemed embarrassed, instead. "Good afternoon, Mr. Barton," he said, "I'm happy to tell you that Limila checked out 100 percent; I can discharge her unconditionally. She'll be with us in a few minutes." Parr smiled; it took him a while to do it. "Would you like some coffee while we wait?" Might as well; Barton did his nod. A young orderly brought coffee; they sipped it, bla-bla-ing politely. I was a bla-bla for the Space Agency, Barton thought.

Then Limila came in, carrying a small suitcase. She wore a sort of turban with earrings pendant from her plastic lobes, a loose-fitting short chemise with contours that indicated Earth-positioned falsies, and half-calf suede boots. It wasn't the greatest ensemble Barton had ever seen in his life, but she moved well in it and his heart sang.

"I can come home now, Barton," she said, "but first I must thank Dr. Parr for what he has done." She turned to Parr. "Doctor," she began, but choked on it. She tried once more. "Doctor. You have made me a person who wants to live again."

Parr wasn't used to raw emotion; Barton saw him trying not to react to it. Barton took him off the hook; he pulled out one of the wigs from his shopping trip.

"Here, Limila," he said, "take that thing off your head for a minute, and try this on."

The hair was long, black and glossy; there was a lot of it. The forehead was in the high range for Earth, but of course nowhere near the over-the-ears Tilaran hairline.

And Limila didn't like it at all. "Barton! This is not me. This is one of *your* women. I do not have hair growing so far forward. You must remember that?"

"It's the highest-foreheaded wig I could find. And it looks *good* on you."

"*No!* I am Tilari!" She tore it away, threw it against the wall.

Barton had had enough. He caught her by the shoulders, taking great care not to grip her as hard as his impulse demanded.

"Now *look!*" he said. "You are on Earth, not on Tilara. You're wearing plastic Earth tits, aren't you?" She looked at him, blankly.

"Tits?"

"*Breasts,* dammit!" Barton relaxed his grip. Limila nodded slowly.

"All right," he continued. "So while you're here you wear the local-style scalp fixtures, too. So that you can mix with people without them staring at you all the time. When we get to Tilara you can do it your way. In fact I'll get a special wig made for you, as soon as I can.

"But meanwhile, Limila," Barton said in a harsher tone than he realized, "you pick that wig up and dust it off and put it on your head, and we will go home."

Nobody said anything. Limila followed Barton's instructions. The wig looked a little mussed, but not badly. Dr. Parr wore a pained expression, as if he desperately needed to visit the toilet but was too polite to say so.

He looked even more as though he'd never make it when Limila went to him and kissed him strongly, before letting Barton lead her away.

In the jeep, Barton couldn't think of anything to say; he was too taken with Limila's new appearance as seen in his peripheral vision. He was embarrassed to look at her directly too much or too often. In fact, he was just plain embarrassed, a feeling that was strange to him. He was glad when they reached their quarters and the ride was over.

He parked the jeep and walked with Limila into the house. Then he asked her.

"The doc's a pretty good guy, huh? Naturally you're grateful to him."

"Oh, of course," she said. "And I had not made love for so long, either."

Before or after the bandages came off? Barton didn't ask; any question would be the wrong one. Tilara was not

Earth, he told himself. But now he saw why Dr. Parr had been so uncharacteristically embarrassed.

Limila was happy, bubbling. She found things Barton hadn't known were in the freezer, and prepared the best dinner he'd had in a long while. She showed him, from the suitcase, two more dresses. Dr. Parr's nurse had helped her order them. She drank with him, bathed with him, and eventually went to bed with him.

First, though, she asked, "Barton, do you want me to wear the wig to bed?" She had it in her hand.

"Suit yourself," he said. "Whatever you want."

"Without it I do not repel you?"

"Hell no!" said Barton. "Look, Limila: one time I was going with a girl who did fashion modeling work. She was quite a doll—long blond hair and a face like an angel with a body to match. One night I went to pick her up for a date, and damned if she wasn't shaved as bald as you are right now. This nut of a fashion designer had her do it, to get some publicity for one of his shows.

"Well, it startled the hell out of me. She wore a wig on our date, of course, but she took it off for bed because she didn't want it mussed up. At first it was odd as hell seeing her with no hair, but after a while I took it for granted; it was still her, wasn't it?" He chuckled. "In fact it looked better on her than the crew-cut stage when she grew it out again."

"But I thought that was part of why you couldn't . . . "

Barton shook his head. "No, Limila; that wasn't it. It was what they had done to your face. I'm sorry I could never see past that, but I couldn't."

"Do you like my face now?" she asked. "It is not as before, really."

"I like it," he said. "It's not exactly as I remember you; no. But it's close enough that it could be, almost. It is you, Limila.

"*Limila!*" he whispered against her cheek, and that was enough talk. Barton didn't get as much sleep that night as he was used to, but he didn't miss it.

Before he went to sleep, it struck him that this was the first sex of any kind that he'd had since leaving the Demu research station. He had not been able to bring himself to love the Demu-ized Limila, and yet her presence, her ac-

cusing presence, had inhibited him from seeking other
women. Well, how about that! Until freed from it, he'd
had no idea how heavy upon him had been the burden of
Limila's disfigurement. He sighed, yawned, and drowsed
off into relaxed slumber.

Limila was nervous, next morning. "At the ship, Barton, what will they think? I am all new. Almost I want to
hide, to wear the veil."

Barton laughed, then sobered. "Don't worry about a
thing. They'll stare, sure. Why not? You're worth looking
at, you know."

"And before, I was not."

Barton went to her. "I'm sorry. It's just that now you're
you again." Then she smiled, and it was all right.

She took as much time choosing between three dresses
as if they had been thirty, but finally chose a white smock.
Carefully she donned and brushed the wig, applied tinted
polish to the glue-on fingernails she was wearing for the
first time. Barton could see that they were not going to be
"bright and early" as Tarleton had specified, but he controlled his impatience.

Eventually they were ready to leave. Barton drove
faster than usual and made up some of the time; they
were about ten minutes late. Tarleton was waiting, pacing
back and forth alongside his car.

"Well, *there* you are!" he said. "I've been—" Then he
saw Limila, and stopped. "Great day in the morning!" He
reddened. "I mean, uh—how do you feel, Limila?"

"Like a person, like myself again. It is not exact, no.
And much you see is artificial. But I see me in a mirror
and want to be alive, not dead. For that I thank you who
authorized that it could happen, as well as Barton and Dr.
Parr." She went to him; before he knew what was happening she pulled his head down to hers and kissed him
soundly. "You see? I do thank you."

"You're—you're certainly welcome." He was redder
than ever. "Look, are we going to stand around out here
all day? We've got work to do."

Inside were only Hishtoo and a guard. Doktor Siewen
was still under Parr's care; old flesh heals slowly. The
guard was new; to him, Limila was a pretty woman, not a

phenomenon. Hishtoo's response was something else; he came forward, stared at her closely and burst into outraged-sounding babble.

Limila laughed. Tarleton looked at her in wonder. Obviously, Barton thought, he'd never heard her laugh before. It did make a nice change of pace.

"He is furious with me," she said. "He says he found me worthy to be Demu, had me made Demu with great effort. Now I waste it and choose to be animal again. He scrapes his hands clean of me."

"He's breaking my heart," said Barton. "I weep big tears."

"Tell him," said Tarleton, "to can the clatter. There's work to do. And that goes for us, too." So they got down to the laborious business of asking questions, of cross-checking the answers they could not trust, against previous results. Hishtoo lied about half the time but his memory was not perfect; he could be caught in inconsistencies. These weren't thrown back at him; that wasn't the idea. But by careful checking, the facts slowly emerged. It was a tedious process, but it was the only game in town. Eeshta, unfortunately, had no technical training.

Barton spent only a short time with them; his main business was with Kreugel, and the ship.

Barton and Limila worked hard for Tarleton that day, the next and part of a third, before his requirements were met. At lunch that day he told them they were cleared to go touring, vacationing.

"Fine business," said Barton. "Is the 12th still on for takeoff?"

"Looks like it," Tarleton said. "Why don't you figure on getting back here by the 10th? In time to check with me and maybe confer a little, that day?"

"Fine by me. Look, would you run through the money thing again?"

The government had reimbursed Barton, by act of Congress, for the value of his lost estate. In fairness he should have received the amount as of the time he had been declared legally dead. But some deskbound nitpicker, by dint of an obscure regulation, had managed to fob him off with the lesser sum that had existed at the time of his disappearance, before the vogue for his paintings. When he heard, Barton said a few four-letter words and shrugged it off. He'd long since forgotten his earlier idea of soaking the government a real bundle for the Demu ship.

He was on an adequate though not lavish salary, and there was provision for expenses when he was off the project site and out into the world; that part had been explained to him earlier, but he'd been preoccupied with other matters and hadn't paid much attention. On the Seattle trip, accommodations had been provided; Barton had spent nothing but a little pocket money. So Tarleton patiently went over it again.

"Your expense-account setup is a modification of the old per-diem system. You draw a flat $100 a day ordinarily. Any week your expenses run over $700 you either swallow the loss or turn in complete receipts if you want to pick up the difference. Up to you. If you're planning to hit any really plush resorts I advise you to collect the receipts. I've put in a special voucher for Limila to get $50 a day. Previously she's been on the books as a temporary ward of the government. You can draw the full advance at the Finance Office this afternoon."

He grinned. "I heard about Groundley trying to give you the runaround yesterday. That was one too many; he's been a nuisance before, and I'd been looking for an excuse to fix his wagon. He's been reassigned to the filing section, so if they can't find your file you'll know why."

Barton and Limila thanked Tarleton, shook hands with him and Kreugel and went home, with a no-problems stopover at the Finance Office. Barton sincerely appreciated Groundley's absence . . .

They made love, packed luggage. Barton exchanged the motor-pool jeep for the rental car he had arranged to have delivered, and they were off and away. Limila was wearing the shortest of the three wigs Barton had bought. It was a short-cut, smooth-cap effect. All were black; Barton couldn't imagine her any other way. It remained to be seen whether she would have a different idea.

She didn't seem to have, when they reached the town and shop where Barton had made his earlier purchases. Mrs. Aranson, the owner, was startled when Barton removed Limila's wig. He borrowed a piece of chalk and drew the Tilaran hairline on her scalp, correcting it to her eventual satisfaction. Mrs. Aranson made sketches, took careful measurements and jotted them on the paper.

"Black and long, like the longest of the three I bought the other day," Barton specified. "And send it here." He gave the lady their address at the project. "How soon do you suppose we could have it? I'll pay extra for speed, because after the 10th of next month is too late."

"There will be no difficulty meeting that date, and no need for extra payment. But with these contours—rather unusual, you must admit—I'll have to design the piece to be held by adhesive at front and back. Will that method be satisfactory?" Limila nodded; she seemed totally unruffled. Mrs. Aranson obviously wanted to ask more questions, but could find no way to do so without breaching her calm professional courtesy.

Barton took her off the hook. "The role in question," he said, not lying, really, "is that of a lady of an alien race, from another planet." Mrs. Aranson smiled. These actors and actresses; they'd do anything!

Back outside, Limila was in a sunny mood. "Thank you, Barton. Now when we come to Tilara I will have other teeth made, also, with the full forty." She looked at him, put her hand on his arm. "But if you like me better as an Earthwoman, then when we are alone I can wear Earth teeth and Earth hair. And Earth *tits!*" Barton broke up laughing.

"Honey, you wear just any little ol' thing you damn please! Or not . . . "

His comment reminded Limila that her wardrobe left something to be desired in the matter of quantity. She shopped rapidly, but it was an hour later when Barton paid the clerk and they were ready to drive on.

They had gone about fifty kilometers further across the high desert plateau when Barton realized he'd forgotten to say goodbye to Eeshta, or to put it to Tarleton that she should accompany the expedition. He made a mental note.

They stopped for the night fairly early. Barton spotted an attractive motel, shortly after they left their narrow two-lane road for an Interstate freeway. After quick showers, they headed for the motel's restaurant.

"We have twenty-two days free and clear," Barton told Limila over dinner, "not counting today or the day we're supposed to get back. Suppose I pick up some maps at the service station. I can tell you what kinds of country we have around here in various directions, and you decide what you'd most like to see."

"That would be nice, Barton," she said. "Can we be among some of your forests, and mountains? And see the ocean?"

"I wouldn't be surprised. Would you like a liqueur with your coffee?" She would. Then they returned to their room, passing the motel pool. In the room, Limila sighed.

"Anything wrong?" Barton asked.

"I would so much like to swim," she said. "I have not swum since Tilara." He started to say go right ahead, and then saw what the problem was. Limila's padded bra wasn't made to fool anyone, under the current styles of swimsuits. Not that many of the swimmers had been wearing suits.

"Excuse me a minute," he said, and went to the manager's office. He noted on the way that the poolside sign quoted a ten-o'clock closing time, and that no one could see into the pool area if the gates were closed. He estimated that by ten it would be getting chilly; they were still in plateau country.

For a hundred dollars the manager was quite willing to close the pool two hours early and turn the gate key over to Barton for the rest of the evening; Barton took a receipt for it. The expression on Limila's face when he told her (he didn't mention the cost) made it well worth while.

Waiting, Barton put his mental note about Eeshta into written form and mailed it off to Tarleton. Then he and Limila swam nude together until the chill chased them indoors, though they'd tried a little mutual warmth in the water. It was fun, but more under the heading of pleasurable gymnastics than true passion.

Three weeks together. Forests and mountains and the ocean; yes. Motels and hotels and ethnic restaurants and miniature 79¢ hamburgers at drive-ins. New Mexico, Arizona, California, a brief journey into Mexico. All the way up the California coast and further to Oregon and Washington. A quick visit to Canada. East into the Rockies, and then south again, back toward the project. Love in the morning, in the afternoon before dinner, and again late at night; nearly every day was like that. Barton knew he was forty but he felt more like twenty. They spent their three weeks' expense money in the first two and forgot to keep receipts; what the hell, Barton's checkbook had his "estate" and accumulated salary to draw on. And once he got off Earth again, he had no idea whether he could or would ever come back. Meanwhile he was having the best three weeks he could remember, ever.

Limila wasn't complaining, either. She *liked* what she saw of Earth, its people and its scenery. Some things must have been greatly different from Tilaran ways; they seemed to puzzle her mightily. Barton tried to explain; she appeared satisfied, usually, with his attempts. Occasionally he asked her about equivalent Tilaran customs, but she shook her head. "You must see; I could not tell you so that you would know." OK; he'd settle for that.

Barton was surprised that no one seemed to notice that Limila's hands were each short a finger by Earth standards. He watched her a lot, the second and third day, and finally saw what she was doing. She had a way of using the fewest fingers possible when eating, say; she'd tuck one or two under, out of sight. Barton didn't ask whether the action was deliberate or unconscious; it worked, didn't it? Barton was all for anything that worked; he always had been. He decided that Parr's cartilage graft, to eliminate the jog at the wrist, also helped conceal the difference.

The first week their free time had stretched endlessly ahead; the second week he put the deadline out of his mind; during the third it rushed upon him like a juggernaut. He ignored it as much as he could. But the night they stopped at a little town in southern Colorado, he was right on schedule. They would reach the project site on the afternoon of Thursday, the 10th, as Tarleton had requested. Part of Barton's mind was damned good at keeping schedules, he decided, even when he didn't want to.

After dinner Barton took the car down the street, to replenish its fuel cells. When he got back, Limila had maps spread across her bed. She looked up at him. "I have been looking to see all the places we have been. May I keep these maps, please?"

"Sure; of course. Whatever you want. Why?"

"You have a lovely world, Barton. I would like these to remember it."

"Oh hell!" he said. "I should have been taking color pics; we could have, easily enough. I didn't think of it. Hey, look: I can order up a bunch of tourist slides for you."

"For me, no need, Barton. Tilarans have full visual recall; we use photographs only to transmit information to one who has not seen personally. Some pictures to show other Tilarans would be nice, yes. I use the maps merely to focus memory on a given sight." Barton made a note to get the pics, anyway.

"Barton?"

"Yes?"

"I have liked Earth; it has been good to me. I wonder if you will like Tilara. It is beautiful, too, but differently. And our ways are very different, you know." Barton didn't know much of anything, he felt, but he'd long since done a lot of guessing.

It was their last night of freedom, of total privacy. Nostalgia for what they had had together made it sweet. Just before sleep they held each other gently. Limila cried and Barton wanted to, and both knew why. For now it was over.

It was a long drive next day but Barton pushed the car, driving faster than he usually did. They arrived at the project early in the afternoon. The mailbox had its quota of messages: Dr. Fox wanted to see Barton; Dr. Parr wanted to see Limila for final routine checkups; Tarleton wanted to see both of them. Somebody was obviously going to have to take seconds.

There was also a box from the wig shop. Limila set it aside, for the time being.

They were unpacking. "Fox can wait," said Barton. "In fact I'd like to dodge her completely, if I could get away with it. Tell you what; let's run over to see Parr. I'll wait; it shouldn't take long. Then we can go and chin with Tarleton."

"No," Limila said, "you drop me at Dr. Parr's and go meet with Tarleton." Barton started to ask a question, but didn't. A special goodbye for lucky Dr. Parr. Well, dammit, the man had earned anything she wanted to give him. And Limila was not of Earth. If that's what she wanted, so be it.

"OK," he said, "I understand."

"Barton," she said, and kissed him. They didn't get away just then, after all.

So he caught Tarleton at the midafternoon coffee break. "Nice trip?"

"Great, Tarleton. Thanks for the vacation; I needed it. Now how do we stand?"

"I hope you're not superstitious, Barton. We've had to allow one day of slippage; Up-Day is Sunday the 13th. It was two days for a while but we caught up one of them."

"Will all the ships come here first? I see only six out there now."

"Four more come here; there'll be four groups of ten each. I couldn't tell you before—it was Top Clam—but the groups are leaving from different bases: here, Seattle, Houston and someplace in Russia they won't tell us for sure."

"Russia? You're kidding me, Tarleton." But Tarleton wasn't. Early in the game the Agency had realized that forty ships were more than the U.S.-Canadian complex could produce within any reasonable time limit. So under top secrecy, Tarleton's superiors had gotten permission to deal quietly, behind the scenes, first with their country's out-of-hemisphere allies, then with the "neutrals" and finally with their nominal antagonists. The result, Barton was surprised to learn, was that the First Demu Expedition would consist of seventeen U.S. ships, seven from the USSR, three each from Britain and Western Germany, and two each from Canada, France, Australia, China and the Greater Central African Republic. Several other countries had pledged at least one ship to the second fleet, given the data and the additional time.

"How in hell did everybody manage *that*, Tarleton?"

"How in hell did you manage to get your ship from the Demu?"

Barton grinned and shook his head. "OK, I get the message.

"Now then. How about me? Personally. Do I get a ship or don't I?"

"You do, in a way."

"What is that supposed to mean? I *told* you—"

"Easy, Barton. You get a ship. But there's been an un-expected development. Of all people, *I* ended up in com-mand of the whole damn fleet!" He grinned. "Some of the military shit green when they heard about that, I shouldn't wonder."

"But what about my ship? Is it or isn't it?"

"It is. Except that you'll have your boss—that's me—riding with you. And maybe looking over your shoulder sometimes.

"Hell's bells. Given the choice, do you think I want to ride with anyone else?" Well, it was a compliment of sorts. Barton poured them both some more coffee. The other man looked ready to go back to work, and Barton had more on his mind.

"Who else rides with us?" he asked. "Limila has to, or no deal. How about Eeshta? Did you get my note about that? And who else?"

"One at a time, Barton; OK?" Barton shrugged. "The ships are built to carry twelve but we're crewing them with ten, all but ours; it rides full. The idea is that if we lose a ship but not all the people, we'll have someplace to put the survivors. You see?

"Standard crew is four qualified pilots, two communica-tions techs and four weaponry artists. Everybody doubles in brass for the other chores. Sound reasonable?"

"OK so far. Now come on with it. What does the Easter bunny have for *me?*"

"All right. You get Limila and Eeshta and you have to put up with me and with Hishtoo. Don't argue; we're go-ing to *need* Hishtoo, somewhere along the line. You know it, if you stop to think for a minute instead of looking stub-born.

"That leaves seven slots. You and three of them will be pilots. I and one other will be communicators. You'll be one short on weapons people. And all of us a little over-stretched, guarding Hishtoo during part of our off-watch time."

Barton thought a minute. "Let me tell you what the problem isn't. Limila is your other communicator, or maybe Eeshta is and Limila is a gunner; we can figure that part out later; it's a long haul. And I see no reason to guard Hishtoo."

Tarleton looked skeptical, so Barton told him. "Nobody guarded him on the trip back here, did they?"

"But he had casts on both arms, or splints, or something."

"Any reason he can't have them on again?" Barton asked. Tarleton looked shocked. "I wouldn't even have to break his arms this time, though I don't mind a bit if you're dead set on realism. Well?" Tarleton still looked shocked; Barton laughed. "I'm *kidding,* man. Hell, all we need to do is keep him locked up."

"I see your point. The Agency figures to give Hishtoo free run of the ship, using some of our manpower to watch him. We may as well not bother their heads about our improved version."

"OK, Tarleton; it's a deal."

Tarleton looked embarrassed. "There's one more thing. I'm sorry, but Dr. Fox went over my head. Her professional standing is such that I can't overrule her in her own specialty."

Barton's guts went cold. "What's to overrule, specifically?"

"She has a red tab on your card and she won't lift it until you take one more test run with her. I hadn't thought we had any problem there, but she seems to have a real bee in her bonnet. Believe me, I'd have squashed this if I could. I need you and Limila both; you've convinced me. And I wouldn't really expect Limila to want to come along if you were grounded."

"No," said Barton. "If that happens, I'll tell you what else will."

Tarleton waited.

"You and the fleet will go looking for the Demu, all by yourselves. You could take Eeshta along by force, I suppose, and Hishtoo of course. But if you took Limila that way she'd never help you find her people. *Or* the Demu. Don't try it."

"I have no such intention. In fact"—Tarleton looked a little sheepish—"I'm going to give you the keys to the car, if that'll make you feel any better. Do you remember that first day, when you handed them over to me?"

Barton remembered. Well, he had picked the right man. "Thanks, Tarleton," he said. "I'll take the keys now, if you don't mind." He got them.

Tarleton wanted to talk some more, trying to give reassurance, but finally recognized Barton's preoccupation and let him go. Still driving the rental car, Barton went home. There was another note from Dr. Fox, this one marked "Urgent." Limila was steaming in a hot bathtub. Dinner was simmering on the stove; it smelled good. Barton fixed a drink for himself and thought about a small woman with a bulldog mind, and about ships, and cages.

Limila came into the room, wearing a short robe and the Tilari wig. She stood before him, waiting for his reaction. Her look was anxious.

A line came to Barton, out of a comic strip from his childhood. "Funny," he said, smiling, "how a pretty girl look good in anything she happen to throw on." Then she was in his lap, and the problem, if there had been one, was over.

During and after dinner he brought her up to date.

"But why do you fear this Dr. Fox?" she asked. "What can she do?"

"She can put me back in a cage, Limila. She has the authority. She can look in my mind and decide that I belong in one, and I'm afraid she will."

"But that is foolish, Barton." He shook his head. He knew that in the back of his mind was something that shouldn't be allowed to run loose. But it would, anyway, as long as he was alive. Determinedly he changed the subject and made it stick.

That night when they made love it was with an air of desperation, and sadness.

The next morning they were cheerful enough, at breakfast and when Barton drove Limila to the ship for briefing. On the way, Barton turned the rental car in to the motor pool and took a jeep in exchange. He and Limila talked, but of nothing in particular. They had a habit of doing that sometimes, he kept telling himself.

Tarleton must have been watching for them; he met them just outside the prefab where Limila usually worked.

"Hi, Barton," he said. "Limila, we have a problem here. Either Hishtoo or Siewen, or both of them, may be getting cutesie with us. And the question is too important to take chances. Come on and we'll run them through it again."

"Maybe I could—" Barton began.

"You go see Fox; she's kicking up a storm," Tarleton said. Then, over his shoulder, "See you later," as he escorted Limila into the building.

"Yeh," Barton said to nobody, "Ol' Indispensable Barton. They just couldn't get along without me." The funny thing was that the incident truly depressed him; he hadn't thought he was quite so touchy.

Well, he might as well go see Fox. It was starting out to be a lousy day; why spoil it? Moodily he drove off in the jeep, kicking up great bursts of dust by gunning it through the more powdery parts of the bumpy road.

Home again, he decided he needed a shower to cool off. He changed into fresh clothes to replace those he'd dusted up so thoroughly, horsing around with the jeep on the way in. He tried to call Dr. Fox and let her know he was on his way. He couldn't get through; the local phone exchange was having one of its own bad days, which were frequent lately. So he set out, unannounced and unenthusiastic.

Barton found himself driving jerkily, and knew the tension was getting to him. He was so close to his goal—so *close*. He felt as though the raw ends of his nerves had grown out through his skin. Normal sensations became almost pain. Everything *jarred*. He forced himself to breathe slowly and deeply, trying to relax, as he parked the jeep and walked to Dr. Fox's office.

Arleta Fox greeted him pleasantly enough. "Do sit down, Mr. Barton. This is Dr. Schermerhorn, our new intern." She gestured toward a bullet-headed young man with a short, scraggly beard. He and Barton shook hands, mumbled greetings, sat.

"I'll be with you in a moment; let me refresh my memory first. This is the latest computer read-out on your overall test series. A quick skim, only, if you don't mind." And what, Barton wondered, if he *did* mind? He recognized the thought as pointless.

Covertly, he appraised Schermerhorn. Intern? He looked more like muscle to Barton; he had the size and weight. Well, we'll see, thought Barton. He hoped he was wrong.

Sooner than he would have preferred, Dr. Fox got

around to him. "Mr. Barton," she began, "I'd like to ask your cooperation in a few more experiments. Brief ones, I assure you." Barton saw her seeing his face freeze, but she smiled and waved a hand as if to mitigate something. "You must understand," she said, "that our basic purpose is to gain some comprehension of the Demu mind, so as to know what our race faces in the future."

"How does *my* head help you with that? You have two for-real Demu, and three people who were bent pretty far in that direction. Plus the ship."

"The study of the ship is in good hands. It is not my province; I deal with living minds. In this case I have very few to deal with, and some are of little use.

"You know as well as I that Siewen is reduced to something of a pushbutton mechanism. His data and logic are intact, but in a sense there is no one home to operate them. He answers questions literal-mindedly, ignoring connotations.

"Heimbach is so disoriented as to be useless not only to me but to himself. Having no access to his earlier records, I cannot tell whether his condition is a result of his treatment at the hands of the Demu, or whether he has always been an incapable personality."

Well, she had those two pegged right, Barton thought. And himself?

"I have had no opportunity to study the woman Limila. I do not like to begrudge you your vacation tour, but I'm afraid I do. Because it eliminated my only opportunity to learn about the mind of the Tilari race. There is no point in trying to perform such a study in only a day or two, I'm sure you'll agree.

"Of the two Demu, we can get only the grossest of behavioral data from the adult. The younger one, on the other hand, is so eager to learn that she is rapidly becoming more like one of us than one of her own race, which we need so desperately to understand."

"Yeah, the kid has come a long way in a hurry," Barton said. "I noticed that."

"So that leaves you, Barton." Well, at long last, she had dropped that Goddam phony "Mister." "You see why you're so important to us? You're the only one who went through the entire ordeal and came out fully human."

(Want to bet?) "They didn't cut you up physically or break your spirit. You are the one who escaped and brought us back the whole package. And I think perhaps you may be the most important part of that package."

"I think you're reading too much into the fact that once in a while somebody does luck out. You already have my head on your computer tapes, along with the story and all my knee-jerk reflexes. What more can you get from me that you don't already have? In my honest opinion, I think you're looking for something that isn't there." He wished with all his heart that he could afford to *have* an honest opinion.

She looked at him, long and hard. "Damn you, Barton! I've analyzed the tapes from that simpleminded computer, and I don't believe the 'freeze trauma' theory any more than you do. I *wish* you would allow questioning under hypnotics. Oh, you needn't worry; I promised not to use them without your consent, and I won't. But you're keeping things back. Not on purpose, probably. But you have valuable data that you won't give me. You can't, because you won't look at it yourself!"

Entirely too close for comfort, lady. Oddly, as Arleta Fox became a greater and greater threat to him, his reluctant liking for her increased. Of course, it was not as though he could let his feelings make any difference to anything.

"I don't know about all that," he stalled. "You could be right; how would I know?" With an effort, he smiled at her. "All right; you must have something you want to try, to get at whatever you think I know that you don't. Or you wouldn't be bothering now, would you? So what's the pitch, Doc?"

"Nothing to worry about, Mr. Barton." *Oh*-oh! Back to the phony deal; watch out. "A few further nonverbal experiments. That is, not written tests; I may ask some questions, of course. May we have your cooperation, Mr. Barton?"

Well, what *could* he say? He nodded.

"Dr. Schermerhorn," she said, "would you show Mr. Barton to Lab B? I'll be along in a minute, as soon as I abstract the notes I'll need, from the file here."

Schermerhorn, doctor or muscle, whichever, politely

showed Barton through a maze of corridors to a door
marked "Laboratory B." He fumbled a key ring out of his
pocket and found the key that fit. Out of the corner of his
eye, Barton noticed Arleta Fox briskly rounding a hall
corner to join them.

Schermerhorn opened the door, and gestured for Barton
to precede him. Barton moved, still watching Dr. Fox over
his shoulder. Then he looked at the room he was entering.

The ceiling was low and gray. The room was empty,
barren, about ten feet square with no other visible openings. The opposite wall lighted; he saw the outline of a
robed, hooded figure.

Eight years hit Barton like a maul. Adrenalin shock
staggered him; he lurched, recovered. Almost in one motion he turned and grabbed the doorframe, kicked at the
door Schermerhorn was closing. The door swung back.
Barton was on his way out. On his way out of the Demu
research station and stopping for nothing.

Schermerhorn was too big, too strong to mess around
with; Barton braced a foot against the edge of the doorframe and launched himself. His head caught Schermerhorn square in the face. Barton landed in the middle of the
corridor, on all fours; Schermerhorn sprawled on his back
against the opposite wall, blood spurting between the fingers held to his face. Instant nose job, thought Barton, getting up. Well, things were tough all over. And the ceiling
back there was low and gray.

Schermerhorn tried to sit up. Barton kicked him under
the ear; he fell back again. Behind him, Barton heard a
noise. He looked around, and suddenly was back on Earth.
It wasn't much of an improvement.

Incredibly, Arleta Fox was still coming toward him.
"*Wait*, Barton!" He shook his head impatiently; there was
no time to waste, talking with a dead woman. He moved
toward her, flexing the hand on which he'd landed much
too hard.

Finally she had the sense to back away. "No, Barton!
It's all right! That was the test!" Yes, I know, Doctor, and
now here come the results. Sorry. But you could be worse
off. You could be in a gray cage.

She had stopped backing now, but was still talking.

Never shut off a source of information while it might still be of use. There wasn't that much hurry.

"Barton, let me explain, *please!*" Oh hell; why not? Barton stopped, but not before he was within reach of her.

"What's to explain?" he said, dead-voiced. "You caught me out, didn't you? Just the way you wanted." The trouble was that he didn't *want* to kill her. She was small like Whnee—no, Eeshta—and female, as he had come to think of Eeshta. And she hadn't harmed him, herself; she had the potential, was all. Suddenly Barton knew that he would not, *could* not hurt this woman. But he mustn't let her know. The hostage principle had got him loose from the Demu; maybe it would keep him out of a cage here, too. If he worked it right . . .

She was still talking; he tried to tune in. " . . . what we needed to know, Barton. Don't you see?"

"Sorry; I missed that. Say again?"

"We knew you were obsessed with something that was blocking communication. We had to find out what it was. It was obvious that you had flummoxed the other tests, but I don't know how and I don't care." She paused. "Well, I do, really, but that can wait. Anyway, we set up this room, as you had described it, and brought you here. That was *it*. You see?"

"Yeh, I see. You found out what I couldn't let you find out. That Barton isn't safe to be running around loose. But here's how it is. Barton is going to run around loose anyway. As long as he is alive, that is." The trouble now was that whatever she might say, he couldn't afford to trust it.

"So right here is where you quit talking and start listening."

He hadn't misjudged her tenacity. She was still trying to talk after he stuffed her mouth full of his handkerchief and tied her gauzy scarf around her face to hold it. She tried to claw the scarf away; he used her belt to tie her hands behind her back. She kicked at him with her high heels; he faced her away from him and gave her a solid knee square in her compact rump, hard enough that her eyes were running tears when he turned her around again.

"Now lookit, Dr. Fox," he said—gently, considering the panic that racked him—"you just behave yourself for a couple of hours until I get me loose out of here, and you can sleep in your own comfy bed tonight and forget all about it."

He looked over to Schermerhorn, who had managed, barely, to sit up. "You, there! If you want to kill this lady, all you have to do is to get on the phone or ring the alarms. If you want to see her alive some more, just rinse your nose and don't do any one more damn thing until she tells you so in person. You got that?" The man nodded, but Barton didn't trust him. There was an easy answer; the door to Laboratory B opened only from the outside. Schermerhorn, with a little help, went inside. Then Barton began steering Arleta Fox down the corridor, hoping he remembered his way out of the place.

He did even better, by luck. He came upon a side exit that opened directly onto the parking lot. In the jeep he fastened the woman's seatbelt and drove away, planning as he went. There had to be a chance or two left.

First he stopped by his and Limila's quarters, locking Dr. Fox in a closet for safekeeping. He packed a couple of suitcases and a grocery bag. He called Limila at the project site.

"Don't say anything, Limila; just listen," he said. "I'll be out there in less than half an hour. Watch for me; I'll be in the jeep. I'll go directly aboard the Demu ship, with all we'll need for a head start. Get loose from whatever is happening and join me *fast*, because then I have to take off in a hurry. You got it?"

"Yes, Barton. But why?"

"They caught me out, Limila. I have no choice. Are you with me?"

"Yes, Barton. Of course."

"Then watch for me, Limila. And be ready to move fast." He retrieved Arleta Fox, led her to the jeep and buckled her in. He set out for the Demu ship. It had served him once . . .

Approaching the ship area, Barton was on the lookout for a possible reception committee. There was none; no one was close enough to notice anything unusual as he hurried Dr. Fox aboard the ship. Relieved to find it unattended, he took her to the control room. It was the best place to keep her, he figured, until Limila arrived.

Almost at once, Limila joined them. He hugged her

briefly, then turned to the doctor. "OK, lady, you can go now." He removed her gag, turned and knelt to fumble with her wrist bonds.

"I *won't* go!" She spun to face him, looking down at him for once.

"Now, look! You're free, you're loose, you're safe. Get your ass *out*." He reached for her; she backed away.

"I *won't*."

The hell with it. Barton stood, grabbed her, retrieved the handkerchief and scarf, and replaced the gag. She scored one good bite on his thumb.

"All right, if you want the Grand Tour you can have it. Here, Limila; hold her, will you?"

It was time, past time, to seal the ship. He did so, returned to the control console and sat down. He inserted the "car keys" assembly.

It didn't work. It just plain didn't *work*.

Well, they had him. Nothing he could do, and no point in taking it out on Arleta Fox, though it had to be her doing. He would have to run on Earth, not in space, was all. But he'd give them one hell of a run, Barton would.

The viewscreen lit: Tarleton's face appeared. Barton hadn't noticed that the ship's switch was on. It didn't matter. What mattered was that his talk with Limila had been bugged. That figured.

"You sonofabitch! You said you were giving me this way out if I needed it!"

"Barton, I was overruled. I gave you the keys to the car. Somebody went over my head and had your drive disabled some other way. I'm sorry; I wouldn't have okayed that."

"Yeh, sorry. I guess you wouldn't. OK, the Agency keeps the ship. I can't carry it off in my pocket."

"Or anything else. A lot of guards showed up here a minute ago, and I'm afraid they have you surrounded. So come on out, why don't you, and talk it over? We can figure out something."

Barton looked at the sleep-gun controls. No, they couldn't have been dumb enough to leave those operational. Of course it wouldn't hurt to try the thing if they went to rush him.

What else did he have on his side? Nothing but a

woman he didn't want to hurt, and in fact couldn't. The bluff didn't seem worth pulling.

"How about a headstart in the jeep, Tarleton? A lousy half-hour, for services rendered?"

"It's out of my hands, Barton. You'd better come out."

The hell you say. Barton said goodbye to himself. He pulled Limila to him and kissed her. Not long; there'd never be long enough. Then he let her go.

"Well, so long, Tarleton," he said. "You were a good guy; luck with the Demu." You have an easier touch than I do, maybe, he thought. Seeing a bare, gray room.

"What the hell do you think you're going to do?" said Tarleton.

"Barton!" Limila cried. "Do not go. You cannot!"

"No," said Barton, "I guess I can't, from here. No place. So I might as well listen to Dr. Fox now, for I don't intend ever to listen to her from inside a cage." He cut the viewscreen and activated the Demu shield. He stood, and removed the gag and bonds from Dr. Arleta Fox.

"So speak up, Doc."

Wearily, he waited for her to tell him what the problem was. His mind blurred.

". . . very ironic, really," she was saying. ". . . in a cage, yes, all those years. Naturally you would do anything—nearly anything—to avoid such a trap again.

"The terrible irony, Barton, has been that your mind is sound as a rock but you wouldn't believe it. Your one great phobia, of course, was being caged. That was the only aspect out of normal range, and understandably.

"So you cheated on the early tests"—she sighed—"and I suppose I'll never know how you did it. At that point you probably were *not* safe to run loose, as you put it. But at the same time you were too valuable to lock up."

Barton's head, he thought, was not only running loose; it was baying at the full moon. He wished to hell somebody would say something that made sense.

"It ever occur to anybody to level with me?"

"How could we? We didn't *know*, because you hid your real self so well." He had to admit she had a point there. Not that it mattered much, now.

"Besides, you wouldn't have listened. It had been too long since you had been able to trust anyone, since you had *had* anyone you could trust." And was there anyone now? Yes—Limila. But what could she do?

"Barton, you came home broken, like Humpty Dumpty. And gradually you have put yourself together again. No one else could have done it for you."

All the king's horses. That didn't make sense, either. Humpty Dumpty was an egg. If Barton was an egg, he was a very bad one.

"I don't know what you're talking about. Maybe you do, but I don't."

"You do, Barton. Think about it: In spite of your hatred, your quite natural hatred for the Demu, you took pity on Eeshta and then befriended her. You stood by Limila when you literally couldn't stand the sight of her—I'm sorry, Limila, but I *have* to make him see—and it was largely your doing that she is as she is now. You—"

Barton shook his head. She'd made it sound good for a minute, but he couldn't buy it. "I threw Skinner through the screen door. Closed."

"That was early on, and he was a nincompoop, besides. But yes, Barton; at that time, before I'd met you, you were one small hesitation away from custodial care. *My* hesitation.

"But—! Aside from guarding your mental privacy, you *were* cooperative. You worked with Tarleton and Kreugel; you worked hard. You trained pilots and instructors. You proposed a plan to bring other races together to help us against the Demu menace. You insisted against all odds upon going back to face that menace again, personally. And when you thought I was the worst possible threat to you—"

Well, she'd had to get to it sooner or later. Now, at last, she was making sense. "Yeh; I busted your muscle boy's face, and kidnapped you."

"He's not a muscle boy; he really is an intern. It was his own fault. I warned him to be careful. But either he didn't take you seriously, or you were simply too fast for him."

"What difference does it make?" Barton was tired, very tired. "I blew it, the whole bit. Let's get it over with. I'm not going back in any cage, is all. Not alive."

For a small woman, Dr. Fox heaved a very large exasperated sigh. "Barton, it is time you stopped being so single-minded. As I said . . . when you thought me the worst possible threat to you, *you still would not hurt me!* Is that the reaction of a man who isn't safe to run loose?"

"I kicked your ass pretty hard, there." Why were they talking so *reasonably?*

"Oh, that! I've fallen harder, at the skating rink!" Her gaze dropped. "Well, almost . . . " Abruptly, she turned to Limila. "Is there any way, do you think, to change the mind of this stubborn man of yours?"

"I do not know, Dr. Fox, but *I* believe you."

She had turned against him! Now they had him almost in a cage, and Limila was on *their* side.

There was nothing left. He had to get out. Where to go? No matter; there had to be a place. Smash Arleta Fox and go!

But she—she was small, and female. He didn't know . . . The walls, it seemed to him, were turning gray.

"Limila!" the woman said. "Help me. Quickly!"

One at each side, holding him, they kept Barton from falling as his knees began to buckle. He shook his head, tried to speak but could not. It was Dr. Fox who spoke.

"Barton, can't you believe that I mean you no harm?"

He heard her as from a great distance, but he felt her pressed as closely to him on one side as Limila was on the other. And now his legs supported him again. His arms came to life; he held both women, fiercely. He looked at the walls, and they were not gray. Not gray at all.

"Shit!" he said. "Barton, you always *were* the dumbest man in the world!"

Neither woman contradicted him.

Two days later, right on schedule, the First Expedition lifted for Tilara. Barton had had Limila give Tarleton the necessary coordinates over the viewscreen before they left the Demu ship, as soon as Arleta Fox had announced all-clear and sent the guards home.

Barton found himself regretting that Dr. Fox couldn't have come along with the fleet. It was a damned shame, he thought, that he'd wasted his opportunity to get better acquainted with that tough little bulldog mind of hers.

She was a winner, that one. And Barton always liked a winner.